Whistleblower

Micheal Romo

ISBN: 978-0-578-83725-3

Whistleblower

This novella is a work of fiction, and no character is purposely to portray any person or combination of persons living or dead.

A terrible plague quickly ravaged the world. Millions died as the disease swept through their bodies, leaving corpses behind. Fear cloaked an entire nation of individuals as they rushed to take cover behind their doors, leaving streets empty. Paranoia began poisoning their minds as they grew frustrated, separated from one another, locked away behind closed doors. Tensions grew as a sense of impending doom lingered in the air.

Then, a single gunshot rang through the country from the east coast to the west. Immediately people rushed out of their homes, filling the vacant streets. They chanted for justice as they burned down cities, leaving them in ash. Fear had morphed into the ugly head of anger, leaving devastation and destruction in its wake. Their leaders did nothing but watch the desolation from their lavished homes, behind nearly impenetrable walls.

CALIFORNIA

Summer was on the horizon; people marched down the streets with signs. They chanted for justice. Hundreds of people walked through the road halting the already gruesome traffic. Nothing could hold a match compared to the crowd's yells, screams, and car horns. A sense of pride flowed through Jack as he zipped through the flock taking pictures with his camera. He admired every picture; it was more than just an image. Each photograph taken was a symbol of beckoning change.

Quickly he repeatedly ran up dividers, mailboxes and, even cars to get the perfect shot. After a few clicks of the camera, he swiftly looked through the photos. He couldn't help but smile. The words 'Change' and 'Justice' rang through his head—the same words frequently chanted by the mob.

News vans and helicopters hover over the crowd moving forward in the street. Watching them were the police patiently waiting for disaster to strike. They stoically stood by their cars, watching as nearly every person screamed in their face or gave them the middle finger. The crowd kept moving forward. They further walked until coming to the center of the street.

Jack looked around, recognizing the expensive shops surrounding them. He'd been familiar with some of the glamorous names above the doors, having walked through, in the past. Finely stitched clothes and lavished cars stood behind frail glass walls. Some shops boarded up with wide planks of wood entirely. A black woman with thick curly hair, dawning dark colors, stood in front of the crowd of people. They stopped in front of her, waiting to hear her preach.

The black woman, who couldn't be any older than thirty-something, darted her eyes at the crowd. She looked at the faces of a skin-colored rainbow. The large gathering before her wore masks, hoping to keep a dangerous virus at bay. She pulled up a bullhorn, putting it to her mouth.

"LET US TAKE A MOMENT OF SILENCE, FOR THOSE THAT WE HAVE LOST." She said through the bullhorn.

Suddenly everyone knelt before her, including Jack. They raised their fist in the air towards her as she watched over them. The sun brightly glistens behind her, shooting rays off her silhouette. The moment was over.

"WE HAVE LOST TOO MANY LIVES. WE ARE

BEING HUNTED! THEY TREAT US LIKE ANIMALS, BUT WE ARE HUMAN...."

The crowd roars with cheers.

"ENOUGH IS ENOUGH! WE MUST FIGHT BACK, NOT ONLY WITH OUR VOICES, BUT WITH OUR FIST. STANDING SIDE BY SIDE IN SOLIDARITY! FOR EVERYONE OF US THEY KILL, WE'LL TAKE ONE OF THEIRS!"

The crowd raves as the black woman stands heroically above them. Two more black leaders behind her emerge, standing side by side with her, looking over the praising crowd. Jack claps with excitement, knowing he was apart of accomplishing good.

Soon the crowd morphed; Jack stood and watched as a small group of pale-skinned individuals walked through the public up to the black leaders. They were submissive in demeanor, hanging their heads low as they nervously trodded towards them. With great intrigue, Jack kept a close eye on them. The light skin group fell to their knees in front of the black leaders, then slowly bent inward, beginning to kiss the leader's warm dirt ridden shoes. The crowd went wild with cheer.

"They have come to repent! This is how we move forward as people. We must forgive each other and ask for forgiveness in return so that we can heal." said the black woman with her shoes licked by white lips.

After polishing the black leaders' shoes with their lips, the light-skinned people looked up at them, with their hands clenched together and tears streaming down

3

their faces.

"Forgive us. Please!" begged the light-skinned people as they wept.

The black leaders looked down at their sobbing faces, their mouths moving into a slight grin. Jack quickly snapped pictures. Standing before the crowd, he knew what he apart of was right. Also thanking god he was half Mexican, so he didn't have to put his lips on dirty shoes. Still, Jack knew this movement was for the greater good.

Nearly at the end of the black leader's sermons, there was a scream that echoed through the streets. Suddenly a stunning white Lamborghini burst from out behind the glass walls. The exotic car quickly dashed through the streets, leaving shards of glass in its trail. In an instant, a row of glass walls shattered into pieces. In a blink of an eye, people were rapidly jumping in and out of stores snapping at the finely stitched clothes, and racing off with the lavished cars.

Jack quickly moved out of the way as a bright orange Ferrari speed through the street, with an entire group of people crammed inside. A police car soon chased after it. Jack found himself engulfed in chaos as buildings started to ignite. He continued to snap pictures as the flames surrounding him grew taller, drowning the streets in a sweltering fire. The police rushed into the streets, trying to contain the madness.

The chaos escalated as people found themselves engaged in combat with police officers. It was the cops versus the people, and the people did not give up without a fight. A crowd surrounded a police officer breaking his bones. Another police officer leaped at an individual, shoving their face into the pavement slapping cuffs around their wrists. At one point, people just flared their arms at each other, friend or foe; Jack made sure to stay hidden in the shadows.

Sirens rang through the air, trying to bring order. Firefighters immediately got to work putting out the fires; water shot out from their hoses. Police charged their way into the crowd capturing as many as they could. Gas popped in the air spreading rapidly. Jack quickly ran to escape towards a ladder on the side of a building.

He kept his face covered as he leaped up the ladder onto an escape balcony. He stood on the fire escape, watching people tear each other apart, like animals. He snapped pictures, capturing their savage like behavior. Jack knew who the real heroes were. The firefighters soon put out the flames but had been too late to save a couple of shops. The riot had quickly died down, scattering with the smoke dispersed, and the cops packing some of them in squad cars. Some officers struggled to shove many rioters into their back seats. Either their car's loaded, or the rioter's pressing their legs against the vehicle. The smoke was clearing, the street once lined with expensive shops was left dilapidated. Shards of broken glass and flakes of ash sprinkled the ground.

2

In his cramped studio apartment, Jack sits down at his desk, typing away at his laptop. He writes an article titled: *Peacefully Protesting Injustice*, and another, *Demonstrators Beaten.* Inspired by the excitement of progress, Jack types nearly endless words of praise. He recounts how heroically the black woman stood, commanding the masses. The brave fight his fellow protestors endured at the hands of the law. Finishing his work, he posts it to his page containing thousands of followers. Within minutes hundreds of eyes click on his articles, then thousands.

Some time passes, Jack lays comfortably on his couch, watching the small television across from him. An unimaginative show about superheroes occupies Jack's attention. Superhero's dominated tv and movies, with usually poor writers and directors behind it all. Suddenly, his phone lying beside him vibrates. Looking down, Jack reads the front of his phone: *Dan Donahue.* He quickly scrabbles for the phone, swiping the call.

Donahue, a middle-aged executive of SNN (Streaming New Network), with frosty blue eyes and a thick brown mustache, appears on the phone.

"Parker!" exclaims Donahue.

"Mr. Donahue"

"Parker, please call me Dan. Listen, I've just gone over the numbers; your articles are a hit!"

"Thank you, Dan."

"I've been reviewing this month's numbers; you've been writing us hit after hit. More people view your articles than any other journalist on our payroll. I like your style, kid; you get down in the deep. You're not afraid to get roughed up, like the rest of those pussies."

"Thank you, Dan. I try to do my best when reporting."

"If only we had more people like you, Parker, you won't believe the amount of the kids that will just plant their asses on a chair and scroll through the internet until a story appears in front of them. We need more people like you, people that'll take a risk-people with balls!"

"Thank you. I believe getting up close, and dirty is how you get the real story."

"Since you're not afraid, Parker, I was thinking, maybe I can send you on a briefing somewhere. Seems like something you'd be able to handle?"

"A briefing?"

"That's right, a briefing. The governor is giving one in the hall of a hotel room downtown. Obviously, not too many people are showing up, but I want someone there to get everything raw. You up to the challenge?"

With slight hesitation, "Sure!" replies Jack.

"Great! I'll email you a pass-just print it out, hang it around your neck, and wear a mask. Get me something good; the governor is a friend of ours."

"Ours?"

"That's right, Parker. You got a problem with that?"

"Uh no, I was just-"

"Listen, my old man once sat me down and said, Danny, if you're going to make it in this world, you got to have a few friends. You want to make it in this world, Parker?"

"Yes"

"Then it's always good to have friends. Remember that."

"All right. Say, Dan, did you have a chance to look at the footage and the pictures of the protest I sent you?"

"Oh yeah, great stuff! That clip and pic of the cop beating that poor son of a bitch on the ground went viral in literally seconds. A lot of people are getting riled up about it. Keep up the great work, kid. I'll send you the pass."

"Thanks"

Dan quickly hangs up. Confidence and relief wash over Jack as he sinks into his couch.

3

Stepping outside of his apartment Jack dawns a blue suit walking towards the hotel, not too far. His camera hangs around his neck, keeping it close. He walks through the shit and trash on the ground. Hardly anybody is driving or walking through the streets of downtown, except for the destitute. They seemed more like forgotten ghosts, left to wander the city aimlessly, some having lost themselves. Life was once on every street corner; now, it seemed like purgatory. Tents lined up along sidewalks with phantoms crawling around them in their madness and feces—all under the watchful eye of a handsome local politician's billboard. A thick fog of sorrow hung over the shanty streets. It was a sublevel of human nature, one where they lived in a concrete jungle surviving off the barren land they once called home.

The sense of poverty had faded away as Jack walked up to the hotel. One miserable beggar perched himself out front, watching few people come in and out. Jack made eye contact with him, though he continued in the building. There nothing he could do; the beggar needed a miracle. They held a temperature gun to Jack's forehead before letting him walk further inside. It beeped; he was allowed in.

Walking into the conference room, only a few journalists stood scattered in the grand hall. Everyone in the room wore a mask. To not wear one was worthy of ridicule and exile. On the front stage stood the governor,

Gavin Bishop. He stands tall and handsome, wearing a beautiful dark navy suit with a matching light blue tie, dark grey hair perfectly combed back, and a magnetic smile beneath his mask. Large cameras surrounded him; other local leaders stood behind him, at a distance. They were plastic ready for the people.

Jack took a seat, his eyes locked onto the governor as he spoke into the cameras. He was a living doll brought to life; he performed so naturally. He was perfect for the cameras.

"...It is with a heavy heart that I sadly report ten thousand more people have died from this disease, that we are all facing today.", Bishop briefly pausing, it looks like he's holding back a tear, almost, "However, we all need to maintain a common strength because this will not be the end of it. Another wave will strike us hard, but we will prevail because we are all united. Together we will overcome this sickness and go back to normal life as we knew it..."

Normal rang through Jack's head. The word that has been tossed around in every conversation on every television, radio, and home. Though what was normal anymore? Jack and many witnessed a siege of protests and riots storming the country as a harsh virus cloaked over it. Normal. The last time Jack thought of that word was when he was able to grab a drink inside a bar. He missed being able to walk into a place, take a break from life, and enjoy a hot meal or a cool drink. That was a different time, before the masks, before people's sanity spiraled away from them.

Bishop stopped talking; he posed for the pictures as the cameras flashed. Jack took a picture before moving up forward for questions. Journalists raised their hands like children. Bishop was ready for them, giving out answers as fast as the questions came flying at him. Bishop waved his finger in the air, landing on a young reporter.

"Governor Bishop, your strategy to put the infected in nursing homes for round the clock treatment may have led to some of the deaths reported. Can you tell us anything about that?" the reporter asked, holding up her phone.

Instantly Bishop replied, "I don't know anything about that. Please next question." His words were like speeding bullets. He waved his finger once again.

"How long will lockdowns last?" another asked.
"Until we flatten the curve of those infected."
"How are families able to provide for themselves with many businesses shut down?" asks another.
"The federal government has sent out checks to every individual that needs help."
"Are you worried about this virus affecting your election campaign this year?" another asked.
"My first worry is the people of this great state; if I prove myself through these troubling times, I'm sure the people will remember me at the polls."

Then Bishop laid his eyes on Jack, aiming his finger right at him. Jack rose.

"With all the chaos surrounding the people regarding the protests, riots, and sickness, what can you tell the American people right now-specifically those that live in California?" asks Jack.

"I can say this, right now, we are all facing difficult times, but one has to walk through hell before reaching heaven. However, we are not alone. Keeping us all in each other's thoughts and prayers will bring us together. We have to make sacrifices, which means staying in our homes, keeping distance between us, for the people's benefit in this great state; until we are told otherwise. 'Till then, my advice is to stay strong; we will get through this and look back at this when we built a stronger unified self. Thank you."

Bishop waves goodbye as he walks off stage. A secretary walks towards the podium, addressing the cameras. The journalists, still restless for Bishop, craving for more. Jack walks off to the side with his job seemingly done, going through the pictures in his camera. Then he feels a looming presence behind him. Quickly turning his back, Jack's eyes meet with Bishop. His height towers over Jack by a couple of inches, and charming features amplified at close range. If he didn't go into politics, he'd been a leading man. Jack is nearly star-struck in the governor's presence. Jack can only see Bishop's eye's squint, but he can feel the man's alluring smile beneath his mask. That's how he won people over, that damn golden smile, that's all he needed to do. Four ape sized men in black suits wearing dark shades stood near Bishop, protective of him.

Bishop introduces himself, "Governor Gavin

Bishop, nice to meet you. Correct me if I'm wrong, but you must be Donahue's guy?"

"Uh-yes, I am. It's very nice to meet you, governor Bishop; my name is Jack Parker."

"Finally, nice to put a name to the face. Listen, just call me Gavin; only my colleagues call me governor, and I must admit it feels damn good!" Bishop laughs, Jack courtesy laughs, "I just wanted to stop by and say hello is all; Donahue told me you got some potential. Judging by that question, I'm sure the headlines will be looking great."

"Uh, yes, you can count on it!"

"Great! Right now, people need someone strong, someone, to lead them through these days of uncertainty. It's all about supporting one another. These days, people helping others is the most important contribution one could make. Besides, we all could use a friend, right?"

"Right"

"Great. Well, nice talking to you, Jack, see you around. I'll be looking forward to that article."

Bishop chuckles then winks at Jack before walking away, with his athletic team of bodyguards behind him. Jack is left mesmerized.

Back in his smothering apartment, Jack sits at his desk, typing away at his laptop, uploading flattering pictures of Bishop that looked more like headshots. He writes the headline reading: *Governor Gavin Bishop, the leader California Needs*. As Jack types at his keyboard, two thoughts stroll through his head, did he believe in Bishop? How vital was friendship? He decided it was necessary enough to complete and upload the article. It was late, nearly morning when he finished. Standing up, Jack steps away from his desk, exhausted, yawning his way to the twin bed shoved in the corner. Jack collapses on the worn-out mattress, his eyelids slowly come down. He falls asleep just as the sun rises, the bright rays peeking through the blinds of his windows. There was no hustle and bustle in the streets below. It was deserted, fit for a hermit lifestyle, where the internet was becoming the new reality. There was only a hustle to get to the computer. It was a lonely window. There, one would log onto an online meeting, devoid of human connection, blocked by a cybernetic wall. This shell of existence was life.

4

A police car pulls into a parking complex to a worn-down apartment building. Two plainclothes officers sit in the front, gathering themselves for a moment. They look at each other silently, nod then, step out of the car. With determination in their eyes, they walk towards the apartments. They scale a single flight of stairs walking to the second floor.

The two officers stand right outside the door to an apartment room. One of the officers closes his eyes, nervously breathing heavily in and out, catching his partner's attention.

"Are you good?"
"Y-yeah, I'm good."
"Stay cool, all right. This guy could be the link to the coke shipments by the movie studios. I need you to be cool on this one."
"Yeah-I'm good-I'm cool."

One of the officers prepares to knock on the door, while the more anxious one stands behind him.

"Police, open up! We got a warrant for a Barry Williams.", the officer says while pounding on the front door.

It's quiet; there's no response. The two officers continue to stand outside the door. On the other side, Barry Williams sits on the couch with his pistol in hand, ready. He looks a little frightened, but nothing he can't handle. Back on the outside, the two officers look at each other, nod, then reach for their pistols and get into position. The more determined officer takes lead, standing in front of the door, his partner close behind him. Suddenly one officer brings down the door with a kick; they rush in guns drawn. Confused by the noise, Barry's girlfriend, Debora, walks out of the bedroom, standing frightened in the hallway. She's immediately horrified by the scene before her eyes. Instantly it's a Mexican stand-off between the officers and Barry.

"PUT THE GUN DOWN! NOW!" yells the focused officer.
"FUCK YOU!, replies Barry.

The officer's partner behind him is a little shaky; Barry catches his itching trigger finger. Just as nervous as the cops, Barry pulls the trigger hitting the focused officer, sending the bullet zipping through his leg, crashing him onto the floor with blood bursting from his shin. Just then, his partner, scared, yells as he rapidly pulls the trigger. Bullets quickly fly in the air. Barry gets

14

winged in the shoulder, dropping his gun, sending him to the floor in pain. Still horrified caught in the crossfire, bullets rip through Debora, killing her. Her corpse collapses to the floor—the shooting stops. The officer snaps out of his fear-induced hazed, still trembling with the gun in his hands. The officer, terrified, examines the room; his partner and Barry spread out on the floor in agony, bleeding out, while Debora lay dead.

"Oh my oh my god," he grabs his phone and quickly dials, "Yeah, send back up quick! Shots fired! We need a medic right now, two people injured!" the officer says, looking around the bullet-ridden apartment.

5

Hundreds, nearly thousands, gather on the streets marching with signs in their hands and dawning black. They yell in anger through the streets, demanding justice. They marched with a beating drum. They hold signs with Debora's picture on it, reading: *Justice for Debora*, below it. They chant Debora's name, along with other slain names. They are like cadets, well-trained moving through the city. The National guard stoically watches over the protestors as they march down the street. They remain calm as some protestors scream in their face shouting obscenities. The guards keep their rifles close to their chest. More chants are echo through the streets. "PIGS IN A BLANKET, FRY'EM LIKE BACON!", "DOWN WITH THE POLICE!" "DEFUND THE POLICE!" the protestors shout as they march.

Trying to capture the best pictures, Jack runs through the crowd. He turns to a protestor dawning all black, covering their face holding a sign. The sign has a picture of Debora below it reading: *SLAIN IN BED, ENOUGH IS ENOUGH!* Jack snaps a photo before continuing to rush through the crowd. Making his way to the front of the public, they all stop waiting to hear their leaders' sermon.

A black woman with two other party members stands with her. The three of them stand before the large gathering of people. They talk through a bullhorn. Their words echo through the street heard by all, taken as gospel. Then the crowd kneels before the three leaders. Some lighter-skinned people walk up to them, begging for forgiveness. Just then, shouting comes from the back; their attention shifts to the national guard that unexpectedly surrounds them. Standing together, the crowd faces the national guard, who have shields at the ready. Tension slowly builds as the protestors shout cruel obscenities while the guards stand waiting. Trash is being thrown over the wall of protestors landing in the cluttering of guards. Suddenly fireworks begin popping off; the guards move forward, thinking it's the sounds of gunfire. The protestors move up, continuing to shout.

It begins, the tensions finally burst with one of the protestors trying to throw a fist at one of the guards but is pushed onto the ground. Suddenly the angry mob of protestors rears their ugly faces swarming at the guards. The guard starts pushing the protestors away from them, trying to arrest some. Protestors shed tears as they feel the cold metal of the handcuffs slap around their wrist. One protestor with a wood plank in hand smacks a guard around the head, only to be right hooked by another guard.

Jack quickly tries to get to a higher vantage point as

16

the chaos begins to suck him in. He paddles through bodies, attempting to reach the sidewalk, where it is clear of any people. A thin blonde girl with pale skin walks up to guards standing their ground. She shouts at them, but they don't give in; instead, they stand coldly.

"Stand back!" one of the guards warns sternly.

"Or the FUCK WHAT?" the girl shouts back, stomping her foot like a child.

The guard says, "Grab her!" swiftly, the guards rope her behind their shields, pinning her to the ground, slapping on cuffs. She screams to the top of her lungs while balling her eyes. Her frightened friends stay back; they only shout at the guards, cursing them.

The protestors fight against the guards spilling blood. Firecrackers go off in the guard's face's cracking the clear shields of their helmets. Guards with their nightsticks in hand fend off the protestors beating them to the ground. Jack standing on top of a mailbox, takes as many pictures as he can. It's absolute madness, any sense of peace or dignity lost. Soon buildings start to ignite once again, flames shoot from out of windows up top. Storefront windows smashed, and businesses looted of all their possessions. Ancient statues have ropes thrown around them and begin to topple, erasing a bygone era's history, breeding ignorance. Graffiti being sprayed, encouraging the death of police and anyone who disagrees. Flames consume entire buildings eating away at their skeletons, turning them into ash as they collapse into rubble.

Jack is taken back by all the chaos around him; he stops snapping the pictures to look at everything unfolding in front of him. With his own eyes, he looks at the power of insanity. The sense of pride that loomed over him at the beginning of the protest slowly fades away. Watching the destruction and brawls in the street, he tries to piece everything together; how it could all make sense in the name of peace, in the name of justice. A thought came to him; sometimes, war needed to rage for justice. He was reeled back in.

Having returned to his apartment, Jack completes an article titled: *Debora Murdered in Bed, Activist Fight for Justice*. Before clicking to upload the report, he stares at his reflection for a moment. He questions his morality, and strangely he doesn't know why. The question dawns over him, compelling him from uploading the article. He makes a decision. Clicking his pad, he uploads it for thousands to read. He walks over to his bed, where he reaches under, pulling out a wooden box.

Flipping the box open, he pulls out a nicely rolled joint. He takes it with him out to his tiny balcony. For a cramped studio apartment, at least he has a view. In the cape of the night, he sits down in a beat-up lawn chair overlooking his neighborhood. Lighting the joint, he puffs smoke into the air. It could be better quality, but it was better than nothing. He begins to lose himself to the flower, diving into his realm. The streets below him quiet without a soul out, except for the poor that roamed endlessly through the city. The emptiness was becoming routine. The sense of loneliness grew on Jack, just like it did everyone else. They all numbed themselves with the bitter taste of booze that soon became sweet or inhaled the potent flower that blew their worries away.

6

Morning, Jack slept on his bed, still dressed in the same clothes from last night. Obnoxiously his phone vibrates, waking him up. With his eyes barely opening, he scrabbles like a blind man searching for his phone, buried in blanket sheets. Finally, grabbing his phone, he rubs his eyes open. Looking at the front screen, it reads: *Dan Donahue.* Jack swipes at the screen. Dan appears, looking refreshed for the day.

"Parker, you look like shit. Did you just wake up?"

"Uh-no, I'll be awake in about five minutes."

"Well, hurry up and make it two because Gavin is giving a speech today on account of last night's rioting or protests-whatever the fuck people are calling it."

"Where at?" Jack asks, releasing a yawn.

"How the hell should I know? You're the journalist; find out. I just need someone on the ground to cover it quick! So far, you haven't let me down."

"All right, I'll get right down there."

"Before I let you go, that article you did last night, it was something. We got over two hundred thousand views just overnight! The best thing, they just keep coming! Excellent stuff, Parker!"

"Thanks, Dan, all in a night's work."

"All right, quit playing cute and get your ass to that speech!"

Dan hangs up. Jack yawns before rolling out of bed. He quickly gets ready, washing his face, brushing his teeth, and getting dressed in his blue suit. All the while, Jack scrolls endlessly on his phone, trying to find out where Bishop will be. Finally, as he gets his equipment ready, he finds out the place, the city hall's front lawn. He dashes out the door with his camera in hand.

Jack hops out of the back seat of a car jogging towards city hall's lawn, where a small group of reporters have gathered in front of an empty podium. Jack joins the small crowd and, at the last second, slips on his mask to avoid the belittling. Two gorilla-sized men in black suits walk onto the stage before Bishop, who waves to the people waiting to hear his homily. A camera crew is ready, with the best angle, getting Bishop's good side. Standing in front of the podium Bishop thinks for a moment before speaking.

Gavin clears his throat, then speaks, "Thank you, everyone, for joining me this morning. To the few in front of me and those watching from the safety of their homes, I want to address last night's demonstration. In the devasting times that we find ourselves in, we must remind ourselves of our rights. Freedom of speech is essential to our way of life and must be protected! The peaceful protest that have been recently active is a reminder that we must fight towards justice, no matter the skin color. Though there were minor instances of violence, for a large part, it was peaceful. These demonstrations are larger than us; it is a struggle against a cruel and unfair system. I have heard the people's voices, which is why I am going to cut down budgets for the police departments. I will also be enforcing more shutdowns on various businesses throughout the county and public activity unless it is for protesting, which is your right. I do this so that all of you may feel safer and protected in this great state. Together we can fight injustice!"

Jack snaps the first picture, which starts a chain reaction of cameras going off. The other journalist instantly raise their voices for questions, but the masks muzzle them. Bishop gives them a charming smile and wave before leaving, brushing them off. The podium now empty the reports leave, one by one. They go on their way, looking for the next story to fit their narratives. Jack examines the photos on his camera before calling for a ride. Suddenly he feels a hand slap on his shoulder. Swiftly turning around, Bishop stands behind Jack. Bishop's light blue eyes locked onto Jack's. Again he can feel that smile, even behind the mask.

"How are you doing, Jack?"

"I'm doing good Gavin, how are you?"

"Oh, aside from the pandemic pretty well. Listen, I saw that article you did on me; I just wanted to say thank you. Donahue was right; you are a good journalist; you have a nice way of writing by actually letting the people in on the scoop. These days, it is such a rarity, and I don't think you're oblivious to that effect, so thank you again. I will say though last night's riot was crazy, the people have spoken.", Bishops says before chuckling.

"Yeah," replies Jack chuckling along.

"Say, I'm having this private event at my house this week, and I want you to come."

"Thank you; I'd be honored."

"Great, we'll get to know each other better and wet our beaks a little. It'll be a great time! I'll send you the invite."

"Thanks!"

Bishop gives Jack a wink before turning away. He

walks away with his guards following him. Jack is left stunned; he's finally in. A few useful articles with detailed photos was all it took. Having a base of eight thousand and counting doesn't hurt either. Jack stood for a moment feeling at peace with himself. There was a little glow of fulfillment that shined deep within him.

Excited, Jack preps for the event. Standing in front of a mirror in his small apartment, he dawns his blue suit, light shirt, and tie. The shirt and tie looked fine, but the actual suit had stains accompanied by little moth holes. The years had not been kind to the fabric. He needed something that would make him stand out in a crowd of somebodies. It was time for an upgrade.

7

A car drives up through the quick loops of the majestic California hills. Charming homes surrounded by tall concrete walls and towering trees stood at the edges. They all had lush backyards, like Eden, and breathtaking views that stretched miles beyond their grasp. Though living here, nothing was out of grasp. Jack had driven through these winding and twisting streets on numerous occasions, always passing through. Every time he stared at these homes, it brought out a sense of remarkability in him. Quickly passing by the grand houses, Jack imagined himself standing in one of their long driveways going into his mansion and resting poolside—the life for a selected few. He played with the thought of being one of those lucky handfuls.

The car finally arrived in front of a modern styled mansion stretching two stories, surrounded by nature. The car pulled up in front of tall gates guarding the entrance to a long driveway. Two guards in black suits stood in front, closely watching whoever pulled up. Jack stepped out of the back seat, dawning his new brown suit, keeping his light blue shirt and tie. He carried a bottle of wine with him to the front gate.

The guards stood coldly at the front gate, staring down Jack through their thick black shades. They didn't say a word. Jack approached them.

"I got an invite."
"You *got* an invite?" said one guard, about to chuckle.

Jack scrolls through his phone before turning it around, revealing his screen to one of the guards. It was the invite, directly from Bishop himself. The guard lifts his wrist, whispering into it. Just then, the tall gate begins to swing open slowly. A man wearing a bow tie and red vest sits in a golf cart waiting on the other side of the gate. Jack walks through towards the golf cart.

"All right, sir, hop inside. I'll get you to the party.", said the man in the vest.

Jack sits next to him. The golf cart zips through the long driveway passing the tall trees surrounding them. The trees begin to fade as it morphs into a perfectly manicured lawn, leading to a circular driveway with a cobble fountain in the middle. The house was modern, very square, very tall. The man kept driving through the front, going under an archway leading to the backyard. The golf cart halts before touching the clean-cut grass. Ahead was an elegant set up of tables draped in cloth, lights, and music. There were few people, all maskless, all rich, all just as powerful as the next. Jack got off the golf cart, starting to feel outmatched. He digs inside his jacket for his mask. Just as he is about to slip it on, Bishop rushes over to him with his bare hypnotizing smile. The pair enthusiastically shake hands.

"Jack! I'm glad you made it," Bishop looks at Jack's mask, "Oh, you don't need that here."
"Are you sure, isn't it mandatory?"
"Yeah, but not here. Come on; I want to introduce you to some people."
"Sure. Oh, before I forget, I brought this wine."
"Oh great, thank you. I'll set it down on the table over there for everyone."

Jack hands Bishop the wine. Casually Bishop gives it to a server, who dashes off with it. Jack brushes it off; it was cheap anyway. Bishop leads him to a group of people. Standing in the small circle is Dan Donahue, Senator Nancy Melosi, activist leader Alicia Ruckus, and famous actress Taylor Milano. Jack is immediately amazed by their presence. He gives them each a nervous hello as Bishop introduces him. Jack had been very familiar with all these people, who never actually met with them, yet their reputations precede them.

"Nice to see you out of the office, Parker," says Dan as he playfully slaps Jack on the back. Jack had forgotten how tall Dan was; he was as tall as Bishop but bulkier. Not very muscular, more fat combined with middle age.
"Jack, is it? Dan tells us you're one of his up and

coming stars; you think he's pulling your leg?" asks Senator Melosi. She was short and fragile-looking, very boney. Her shark-like eyes nearly popped out of her head. She shook as she stood; maybe it was the cracking old age or the heavy drinking.

Jack nervously laughs before answering, "I hope not."

"I'm sure he'll do fine. I've read some of his work; it's not bad at all," adds Alicia. She was taller than Melosi, a young pretty black woman who was sharp on her feet. She wore a lot of black clothing, probably for the cause she leads. It felt like every stare she made was another calculation in her head.

"Thank you; it means a lot coming from you. I've been attending as many protests as I can."

"Well, that's good. The good fight is always worth fighting for. Taylor and I were just discussing the low opportunities for people of color in the entertainment industry." replies Alicia.

"Oh yeah, there's just too many white people in the industry-sometimes I feel like I'm walking around with ghosts," says Taylor.

They all laugh, except Jack, who hesitates before joining. He finds her joke ironic; her skin is pale, complemented by her dirty blonde hair and frosty blue eyes. She's tall, nearly passing Dan, also beautiful though skinny and lengthy. Jack had seen her play as a superhero on the big screen when the theaters were open. Now she sang about politics.

"You know I'm glad that all of us are in this fight together. I think it's always a good sign when people can unite on a common goal, for the greater good. Jack's articles have been a tremendous amount of help.", says Bishop.

"Yes, they bring to light the big issues; people can't get enough of them. The numbers speak for themselves, and they get people talking.", adds Dan.

The six of them continue to talk and drink. A few drinks later, they find themselves sitting around a table, looking at each other as they speak.

"You know, it's so easy for people to look at the violence during these protests. What many people don't realize is that, for there to be change, sometimes there need to be some drastic measures taken.", says Alicia.

"I don't get how people can be against it. There is a serious issue in this country that needs to be changed. I know. I will never understand any pain or suffering that a person of color would go through, but every day all I can do is try.", replies Taylor.

"That's all we're asking; some people just don't get it."

"I understand where you're coming from, Alicia. I-I mean voter i.d. is just the most insulting thing for a person. Some down and out folks d-don't even know w-where t-t-the DMV is or have access to the internet. People just don't understand.", replies Nancy, already drunk sipping her fifth or sixth glass of champagne.

"Well, I can tell you the protests have generated good buzz on the news floor. We support it, and people love it. Jack can tell you all about that. He brings them in.", says Dan breaking his eyes away from his phone, interjecting in the conversation.

Alicia darts her eyes to Jack.

"What about you, Jack," Alicia asks.
"About me, what?"
"What do you think about all the protests and the movement?"

Jack hesitates slightly before answering quickly, trying to gather the right words in his head. Alicia looks at him suspiciously, waiting to hear his response. It's as though Jack is going through some oral test.

"Well, I think it's a good start. I've been to many peaceful protests, covering them on the ground, giving my support. I think if they continue, we'll see change heading in the right direction. You'll certainly find me there too."
"I'm glad to know there's nothing but friends here supporting one another. If only the rest of the country got the memo, then we'd be halfway to building this country as it should be."

Sitting around the table, they all drink more wine, slowly getting a buzz. They drink some more and laugh. Jack throws down the expensive red wine. He can taste the difference between the average ten-dollar wine he's used to and the soothing red he pours down his throat. He's not sure if he can go back; maybe he'd take a bottle before leaving.

Some more time passes along. Jack, now alone with an empty glass in his hand, wanders around the beautifully manicured backyard. He marvels at the elegant decorations set up all around him. Walking a little further, Jack casually sets his glass down on a table. He goes towards a balcony with a breathtaking view of the city. He stands on the edge of the balcony leaning on the rail in front of him. His eyes stare at the city's towering skyscrapers against the backdrop of a sunset slowly coming down behind purple colored mountains. It was all laid out in front of him like a painting. Suddenly everything he knew about the city was gone; all the slums and bums were wiped from memory. From where he was standing, everything seemed within his grasp. Everything made sense to him. Rushing through crowds of people, taking picture after picture, writing countless articles until morning. It all made sense; it paid off. He did what he was told and made some friends along the way. Things were looking bright; he could see it in the distance. The sun was diving deeper behind the mountains. It wasn't just a sense of pride that washed over him, but a sense of belonging. It was like Jack was standing on the casino floor with a hot streak, only he wasn't going to let it end. He turned to look at the crowd behind him; they indulged in their refined atmosphere, basking in their power.

Turning back to the city, a glowing, moving street off in the far distance catches his eye. He squints his eyes, trying to get a more precise look. He barely makes out the shapes of hundreds of people marching down a street—another protest. Something came over Jack as he towered over the protestors walking down the streets with their signs in hand and their chants echoing.

"Isn't it a sight?"

Jack turns, an alluring woman has popped out of nowhere, now standing beside him admiring the view. She didn't look that much older than Jack, maybe a little younger in her early twenties. Her skin looked smooth, and her light complexion enriched her pale pink dress. She had dark brunette hair with a slight hint of blonde. Her emerald eyes matched her soft nude lips. Jack didn't even know such a woman had existed. She was something out of the front page of a beauty magazine. She was elegant, confident, sexy, and mysterious, all wrapped together. There was a warm passion in her eyes. She didn't look like the type to give any guy the time of day. A select few, sure. Jack thought, maybe he could be the few. She was like magic, a magnetic mystery waiting to be revealed. Hundreds of thoughts ran through Jack's head. Not one of them the answer to her question. She had him; she didn't even know it.

"I'm sorry.", replied Jack trying to hide his fluster.
"The view, it's pretty, right?"
"Oh yeah, it's nice."

Silence falls between them; Jack can feel her slipping away. They stare at the view while Jack tries to think off his feet of something worthy to say to get the conversation going. Finally, it came to him; it was better than nothing.

"I don't think I saw you earlier in the crowd."
"Oh yeah. The thing about crowds is, they aren't my thing."
"You don't like crowds?"

"I like to think of myself as a lone wolf type. What about you, you a crowd-pleaser?"

"What?"

"Yeah, you the lone wolf type, or do you run with the pack?"

"I don't know; I've never really given it that much thought. I guess I like the idea of other people."

"Yeah, always sounds good in the beginning; that's how they get you. Then you start getting to know them; soon, you know exactly what type of people you're dealing with. Some say we all have three faces; let's just hope none of them are ugly.", she chuckles. Jack chuckles with her.

"That's pretty insightful."

"Really? You think I'm insightful; you don't even know who I am."

"Okay fine. You're pretty self-aware, which means you got to be smart on some level."

The pair chuckle, looking up from their drinks, they smile at each other.

"My name is Lisa.", she says while extending her hand.

Jack dives for her hand, shaking it as he replies, "Jack."

"So, what brings you here, if you're not interested in crowds so much."

"It's more like who, a friend who told me this would be fun. Now I like to think I'm pretty optimistic, but this wasn't exactly my idea of fun. Though it beats staying cooped up in a house all day."

"What's your idea of fun?"

"You like drives?"

"Drives?"

"Yeah, have you ever gone out for a long drive and felt the wind pass through you as you hit the pedal? It's one of the most relaxing things in the world."

"I don't have a car, so I wouldn't know."

"You're kidding, you live in Los Angeles and don't have a car? You're a mad man. How do you get around?"

"Car services and trains haven't failed me so far; it's not too bad."

"You want to go out for one now?"

"Right now, right now?"

"Are you deaf? Yes."

Jack wanted to say yes instantly; he could feel the words on the tip of his tongue. Just as he is about to let them out, an image of Bishop comes to mind. With all the friends he's made, Jack feels a tether from the crowd. He stares into Lisa's eyes just a bit longer; then, a weightless feeling hits him.

"All right, let's do it, let's go."

"Yes, cool! Follow me."

Jack follows Lisa to the front of the house. He walks past the party, still raving with people laughing and waving their drinks around. Following Lisa, Jack didn't feel like he was missing out on much anymore. He thought he'd miss a lifetime if he said no. The pair hop onto the golf cart and zip back to the driveway.

Jack sits beside Lisa as she sits behind the wheel of her 911 Porsche. In her convertible, they feel the wind splash against them as they drive hastily through the mountains. Lisa commands the wheel with a sense of relaxation as a smile stretches across her face and hair blowing in the breeze. Jack, though trying to put on a brave face, clutches the handle of the car door. He can't help but feel his heart drop every time they speed past a loop. Moving through the mountains, Jack looks down at the vast nature resting below him, untouched and peaceful. The sun left the sky with just a ray of light sticking out from behind the mountains in the distance. Lisa eases on the gas pedal as she pulls into a small plot overlooking the vast nature on the other side of the mountains; it was unprovoked by man's touch. They sit in the car, Lisa gazes into the distance. Jack can't keep his mind off her; his eyes gravitate towards her at every turn.

"I've just realized something.", says Lisa.
"What?"
"I hardly know anything about you other than your name."
"Okay...what would you like to know?"
"What do you want to look back on when you're old and shriveled and be able to say, I did that and got it!"
"I guess I just want to make it."
"Well, that's obvious-everyone wants to make it, but what does that even mean?"
"I don't know, maybe be somebody. Not live in a sardine can for an apartment, have nice things, maybe for everyone to get along, I guess."
"Is that all you want is nice things and peace? Nothing else?"

Jack leans in a bit closer, "I can think of something

else.", he says as he puckers his lips. Then he feels something gently press against his mouth, opening his eyes. Lisa has her finger pressing against his lips. She's amused, chuckling a bit. Embarrassed, he pulls away, staying to his side of the car.

"It's okay, valiant effort though.", says Lisa as she continues to chuckle.
"All right, what about you?"
"Me?"
"Yeah, you."
"Okay, let's see, I want...I want a plot of land somewhere far from the city. Where the air is fresh, and there's nothing but wilderness around you. Where I can be left alone from people and find some peace."
"You don't like people?"
"It's not that people are fine. It's just when you're cooped up together all the time-well people just drive each other mad."
"So, you just want to be left alone. You don't think you'll be lonely?"
"A person can be just as lonely even in a room filled with people. Besides, I hope to have a family one day anyway."
"That doesn't seem bad. Actually, it sounds kind of pleasant."
"Some people think I'm a little crazy for wanting something like that, but I just don't think they're in the loop yet."
"I don't think you're crazy."
"Really? That's good. You probably wouldn't want me behind the wheel if I was."

They both chuckle, then Lisa rests her head on Jack's shoulder. He's instantly taken back by it but

33

remains calm as he wraps his arm around her. They both look off into the distance under the cloak of the night with the stars twinkling above.

Driving down the mountain back into the city, Lisa pulls up in front of Jack's apartment building. He regrettably gets out of the car then immediately turns to Lisa, who smiles with soft eyes.

"Let me take you out.", says Jack with a hopeless smile on his face.

Lisa's smile morphs into a chuckle; she looks away for a moment before turning back to look at Jack. He stays optimistic, but his gut tells him otherwise.

"Listen, Jack, we had fun, but there's something you should know. I'm a hard one to catch."
"That's okay. I'm a good catcher."
"Tell you what, if we see each other again, ask me."
"Great! When can I see you again?"
"I said *if*. For now, let's see what happens. We bumped into each other once. Let's go for two. Goodnight."

Lisa blows Jack a kiss before stomping on the gas pedal, speeding down the street. Jack chuckles before nodding his head, walking up into his apartment.

8

Javier Valéncia stands proudly in front of a small television crew as they get ready to interview him. He is not afraid to be maskless, revealing his charismatic smile. He dawns a deep navy suit, blue dress shirt, and bright red power tie. His raven-black hair turning grey well combed. His dark mustache curled at the tips giving off a sense of intimidation, yet he seems friendly enough. His campaign crew stands behind him. Beside Javier stands his poise and loyal wife, Maria. She is fashionable, wearing a refine summer dress, though she wears a mask. Javier greets the crew with a smile, ready to take on the reporter's questions.

The one reporter asks a question, "Mister Valéncia, how do you feel running against Governor Bishop, who has held his position over two years now."

"Well, I have to say I'm disappointed with the way the governor has been running the state. I think if the people found out a little bit about the issues I'm running on, I think they'll realize that I would be a better fit."

"I've noticed you aren't wearing a mask. Are you not concerned with the virus that is spreading throughout the country?"

"I don't wear a mask because I want people to look at the face of someone fearless, during a time when fear seems to be heavily pushed as the norm. People need to see the face of who they are thinking of voting for."

"Going back to the topic of the virus, is it true that you would bring an end to the lockdowns currently in place? Aren't you concerned about the safety of people?"

"I'm concerned about the people of this state! More than Bishop. Look, right now, I can walk down the street and see businesses closed. People rely on those businesses to keep them from going hungry, to keep a roof over their heads. These lockdowns are hurting people more than the virus. So yes, I do think reopening businesses is a good idea. And for the safety of the people-look, it is their choice, there is a point of trust, and I can't legislate an individual. People have to be able to make calls on what's right for them and their fellow citizens.

"I see, well, just a few more questions. The border is close to our state and has become a pressing issue over the last few months; the people would like to know, what is your immigration policy."

"My policy is, ship them back! You don't have to hold them, just ship them back. We can't keep receiving people. We need to work on ourselves here first. They bring a lot of trouble, and right now, we have enough trouble in our state to deal with as is."

"There has been discussion about your religious beliefs. Is it true you're a devout Christian?"

"Yes, I practice my belief just as anyone else would."

"Are you going to lead with your belief?"

"I feel like I'm being integrated here," Javier laughs, "I'll lead with my conscience. I have a good one; you'll be in good hands. Thank you for your time."

Javier waves at the camera before turning away, walking towards his wife holding her hand; they walk to their black tinted car, waiting just behind them. Javier's campaign crew quickly follows him. His private security, tough guys dressed in dark suits, make sure he gets in the car safely. The small television crew film Javier and his team, loaded in their black tinted vehicles, drive away.

Elsewhere on the SNN news program set, an anchor begins reporting the news solo behind a desk. The anchor was an older man, white, clean-cut, dressed in a sharp suit, wearing black-rimmed glasses. The cameras start rolling; the anchor looks directly into the camera.

"During an interview today, California native real estate mogul turned governor candidate, Javier Valéncia refuses to wear a mask, encourages the reopening of business midst a deadly pandemic, and says immigrants are trouble.", says the anchor sternly, as though warning the audience.

The news then plays edited clips of Javier during the interview. He is shown to have said, "I don't wear a mask-people need to see the face of who they are thinking of voting for." Which cuts to, "I think reopening the businesses is a good idea-for the safety of the people." Then cuts to, "My policy is ship them back! They bring a lot of trouble, and right now, we have enough trouble in our state to deal with as is."

The screen cuts back to the anchor, he continues, "Some find the candidate's words controversial and think this could affect him on the campaign run. Joining me to discuss this is a political science professor from Harvard University, Al Medox." Al Medox, a dull, middle-aged, balding man, who probably lifts more outdated books than weights, appears on screen alongside the news anchor.

The anchor starts, "Thank you for joining us tonight, Professor."
"Thank you for having me on your program tonight."

"I was wondering what you can analyze from the political discourse that is going on with the candidate, I mean, he seems unsympathetic, and some suggest even very problematic."

"You know he is, but this behavior from the candidate does not surprise me, given his other interviews displaying little to no courtesy. I think he is going to have a tough time winning over the people of California, especially with him putting people's lives at risk."

"His plan to reopen businesses does seem dangerous and could lead to more deaths."

"It definitely could! Valéncia's plan is very irresponsible behavior and should be condemned. He is not following the science, which states that people need to be separated at this time! We need a leader who pays attention to what the experts are saying, for everyone's benefit."

"His immigration policy seems unnecessarily aggressive, almost like a call for violence?"

"It does. In political science, one would learn it is best to choose a sympathetic candidate to hear the people's voices, keeping democracy intact. Judging from the interview, I don't think this candidate cares too much about keeping democracy intact. I think he might as well just be calling for violence."

9

A car swings into an affluent neighborhood, stopping in front of one of the majestically designed homes. It's a tall, charming colonial home with a white picket fence and freshly cut grass. Jack steps off the car, walking towards the front door; he wears the same brown suit from the other night. He knocks on the door. A moment later, a maid opens the door. Jack politely waves, walking in; the maid says nothing, greeting Jack with a silent smile. She walks away, going up a carefully crafted staircase. Jack stands alone in the foyer, looking around, immediately impressed. The entrance alone is more spacious than his entire apartment. A glass chandelier hangs above him, twinkling. Perfectly taken family photos hang on the walls. Then Dan walks out from a room, going down the flight of stairs grinning at the sight of Jack. The pair shake hands.

"Parker, glad you can make it!"
"Thank you for inviting me. You have a beautiful home, Dan."
"Thank you, Parker, maybe one day you'll wise up and ditch that sardine box of yours. Come on up; we got business to discuss."

Dan walks Jack up the stairs, reaching the second floor; it was just as beautiful as the first. Dan guides Jack into a room. It's Dan's home office, a sophisticated designed room with expensive wood panel walls, bookshelves stretching to the ceiling, filled with many books, comfortable leather seats, a handsomely carved desk, and a flat-screen hanging on the back wall. A true intellectual's room. Dan takes a seat behind his desk; Jack takes a seat. Turning around, Dan turns on the television; they watch SNN. The segment is commentary; all focused on Javier's latest interview.

"What an asshole.", Dan says with his eyes glued to the screen. He then quickly turns to Jack, "Have you seen this guy?"

"Yeah, I was reading an article; it's the opposing candidate...Javier Valénica, right?"

"That is right, Parker."

"So, what did we need to discuss?"

"I was looking at the viewership numbers and noticed something pretty interesting. People hate this guy, but they love to watch him!"

"What does that have to do with me?"

"Well, Parker, I invited you to my home because I think it's time for you to move up in the world. I'm giving you a promotion."

Jack's face instantly lights up. Dan looks at Jack, amused, his mouth grinning.

"Thanks, Dan, I really appreciate this!"

"I know you do, kid. It's exciting; I remember when I was moving up in the company. I felt pretty damn unstoppable. Now, let's get down into the details of the promotion. I'm assigning you in charge of a team to get all and any information on Valénica."

"All right, sounds easy enough just to follow a candidate."

"Well, there's something I feel like I should clarify before we finalize everything. I want to ask you, how do you feel about Javier Valéncia?"

"I'm not sure how I feel about him. I haven't seen a whole lot from him. However, from what I have seen, I don't think he'll make a good governor for the state."

"How do you feel about our friend Gavin?"

"He's a good guy; I think he's doing a good job; he cares about the people."

"That's good, that's real good. I want you to keep all that in mind as you're conducting your work in this team."

"So, you just want us to lean towards Gavin, is that it?"

"Look, Parker, we're all friends now. Do you know what friends do? They watch each other's backs. I've got you, and you've got me, and we both got Gavin."

The excitement in Jack soon washes away. The realization of what is happening hits him. He's struck with silence. He tries thinking for a moment, trying to find the right words. Millions of thoughts race to the front of his head all at once. He rises from his seat and walks over towards the window. Looking out, he tries to put his thoughts together. He notices Dan's kids play innocently in the manicured backyard. The two little brothers run around chasing each other, laughing. Dan follows Jack to the window; he looks at his eye contact.

"That's Sawyer, and the taller one is Nathan."
"How old are they?"
"Sawyer is seven, and Nathan is about to turn eight."
"They look like good kids."
"They're the best."

Dan stares away from his children, now to Jack. He's got Jack's attention.

"Listen, Parker, I know what I'm asking you to do isn't the best thing in the world, but this guy running for governor, its trouble. First, it's him; then there's someone worse than him that's going to come along. You got to think about them," Dan says, pointing at his children, "They're the future; do they really get one from a guy like Valéncia? Someone who seems so full of themselves they don't know the job at stake?"

"We don't even know how bad this guy is."

"Think about it, if this is him now, imagine him towards the end of the election. Imagine him in office with all that power. I'm asking you to do this is for the greater good; trust me on this. I chose you, Parker because you've got people that listen to you; you got what these journalists out here lack, balls! I need someone like that to help me out, not just for me, but think about the people of this state. What do you say?"

Jack thinks for a moment; his mind splits into two heads, debating one another non-stop. It feels like hours have gone by as he takes a moment. Finally, Jack looks up into Dan's eyes.

"All right. I'll do it."

Dan's smile stretches wide across his face. He pats Jack on the back then brings him in closer, wrapping his arm around his shoulder.

"You've never disappointed me, Parker. I already got a team together for you; I just needed a commander. You start tomorrow morning at five; meet them in the office."

"I thought it was closed because of the virus?"

"You're an important leader now, special privileges.

Besides, it's a small team in a near-empty building anyway, so you'll be fine. Come tomorrow, ready to lead, all right?"

"Yeah, okay."

"Oh, and hey, this promotion means a little bump in pay raise. So, keep making the right moves, and you'll be out of that matchbox you call an apartment in no time."

Dan laughs, Jack chuckles, playing along.

"How much is the raise?"

"What'd you make now?

"Thirty thousand?"

"That's about right. We'll add fifty; how's that sound?"

Jack's jaw nearly drops. Dan's amused; it's petty cash to him.

"That's great!"

"I knew you'd be happy. Oh, before you head out, I need for you to sign some papers."

"Papers?"

"You're an essential worker now; it's time to make it legit."

Dan walks Jack over to his desk, where he pulls out a paper from his drawer. Jack stares at the contract lying below him, the moment of truth. He can feel the form staring back at him. Suddenly, a heavyweight feeling collapses onto Jack; his mind races in circles once again. Dan holds a pen towards him. Jack reaches for the pen, it's, in his hands, clicks it. With the pen in hand, Jack

43

brings it down towards the paper. Everything seems to be moving slower, as though time were at a standstill. Finally, he was getting recognized for his work; all the pride he felt covering stories, uncovering the truth was about to pay off. Or maybe he was fooling himself into believing he deserved this. He thought for a split second perhaps he hadn't delivered the truth; he was just like the rest of them, wanting it big, sacrificing himself.

Suddenly, before Jack could think further, his hand already signed the paper for him. The deal was done. Dan chuckles in excitement, swiping the contract off his desk, holding it up, admiring it.

"You've done yourself a huge favor Parker."

Jack doesn't say anything but silently drops the pen onto the desk. Dan looks at Jack, very much pleased.

"Listen, now that you're a big shot, why don't you get yourself some wheels. You're a leader now, none of car service bullshit. Go get something nice; lord knows you can afford it."

Jack is speechless; he doesn't know what to say or how to feel. He emotionlessly looks at Dan with a light smile.

"Yeah-okay," Jack replies.
"All right, good work, be at the office tomorrow at five; your crew will be waiting."

Dan slaps Jack on the back-patting him. He couldn't be prouder. With his mind still, adrift Jack shakes hands with Dan before leaving his home.

10

Jack walks through a car dealership. Every car on the lot is just as luxurious as the last. He admires the vehicles up close; still, in disbelief, he can now actually afford to buy one. Then a particular ride catches his eye. It's a slick, all-black, two-door BMW. Jack stands in front of the driver's side, peering into the window, glimpsing back at his reflection. A hand reaches for the door handle pulling it open. Jack turns around to face one of the car salesmen, who probably had been stalking him before.

"Would you like to have a seat?" the salesman asks.
"Sure."

Jack swings inside the front seat, sitting down in comfortable leather burgundy seats. The car's entire interior draped in burgundy and black; the car gave off the power. Jack felt that same power as his hands soon gripped the steering wheel. The salesman slowly smiled as he realized the car's seduction had been working its magic on Jack. With a smirk on his face, the salesman thought of a new hook.

"Why don't you press that button on the right." said the salesman. He nods at one of the many buttons inside the car.

Jack presses the button, then the top of the car raises then comes down in the back. Jack felt a specific control wash over him as he sat in the luxurious vehicle. He knew right there this was going to be his car.

"So, I can tell more about this vehicle if you'd like or if you want to try it out for a test drive, I can have that arranged-"
"I'll take this one."

The salesman looks at him, shocked, but Jack just grips the car's wheel and already feels the engine's vigor.
Jack finally purchases the car. Sitting behind the wheel of his fast and sleek new BMW, Jack races out of the dealer lot. He drives through the street, zipping along the lanes passing every car coming his way or in his way. He's a mad man behind the wheel, but he's in complete control. The wind rushes through his face as he races through the streets without a care in the world. He'd felt different; now, he'd felt things were in place for him. It was all coming together.

11

Jack quickly pulled up into his reserved parking space. Then he made his way towards the office. It was one of the few tall skyscrapers in the middle of downtown; Jack went inside. As Jack stepped into the elevator, he was ready for the day. He wore his new striking black plaid suit, white dress shirt, and matching dark tie, making him a force to be reckoned with. After a few moments of standing, the doors finally opened. Jack walked into the newsroom, the old office, now seemingly abandoned, except for the conference room in the middle of the floor. Its glass walls make it stand out on a floor filled with empty desks and cubicles. Jack walked into the room, leaving the door open behind him. His team, a small group of recent college graduates wearing masks, sat around the table staring at him. Right off, they seemed timid. Jack was surprised for a moment, thinking he was getting more seasoned reporters. He hesitantly stands at the head of the table, staring down all the young fresh faces around him. He was only twenty sevens years old, but the group around the table made him feel like a man of fifty.

Jack started, "Okay, I'm glad that all of you can make it this morning. I understand that you were each informed what kind of reporting we'll be doing here. So, who would like to start us off?"

Jack takes a seat at the head of the table. He looks at the perplexed faces of the youth in front of him. They each turn to one another, expecting the answer to suddenly burst out of one of them. Jack continues looking around the table, waiting for one to have the guts. At least if they had nothing, they could say something-anything. Then he decides he's waited enough.

"All right, since nobody wants to go, what about you?" Jack said as he pointed to a blonde girl near the end of the table. He only picked her because her bright red glasses stuck out, they looked kind of stupid, but she pulled them off.

It was like the girl had a mini-stroke; she had a little panic before freezing up. Then slowly, she started to say something.

"Well-uh, I...um...I took a look at what the candidate

Valéncia said; people are really riled about his views on the social programs in the state.", the blonde girl said mousy.

"All right, we're off to a good start! What was going on with the social programs?"

Then another one of them spoke up, a young black kid closer to Jack, said, "Well, I was reading that he wants to completely cut a lot of social programs that the state has to offer. One of the programs being about climate change. I guess he doesn't want to ban gas guzzlers."

"Okay, good. Before we get ahead of ourselves, let's start with some basics; what are your names?"
"Julius Redbock," replied the black kid.
"Holly Smith," said the blonde.
"Okay, I want to hear from someone else around the table; come on, speak up. We're on a roll."

An Asian girl with kind eyes, who sat near the back, spoke up, saying, "Well, some people seem to like that he plans to reopen a lot of businesses even though we're in the middle of a pandemic. But there's a whole lot of people who don't like it either. They seem to be pretty split on the decision."

"All right, let's keep this going; your name?"
"Zoey Chang," the Asian girl replied.

A white kid, who looked like he'd never seen a weight in his life spoke, "Well, some people are starting to question his taxes. Apparently, he didn't pay them all. My name's Zack Milton.

Jack rises from his chair; he takes control of the room.

"Javier Valénica, what do we know about him? He's a successful real estate mogul. What else do we know? He wants to cut social programs, reopen business during a deadly pandemic, taxes are in question. I took a look at his opinions on the border between this state and Mexico; he wants it closed, send them back, he says, they're trouble. Self-hating. Does this man seem like the right man to lead this state?"

The youth sitting around the table look at Jack, confused for a brief moment before shaking their heads, no.

Jack continued, "Then it is our job to inform the people of this beautiful state that this man is not the right one for the job! If he were to be in office, people would suffer. Our man is Gavin Bishop. He's the right man for the job; he cares for the people of this state. He understands them like he did after the protest broke out and supports locking down everything until it is safe. He understood that there is a fight against inequality, not just in this state but in the country. Now this other candidate steps in, I don't know if his intentions are as wise as Bishops. These are the stories that we need to be covering. I mean now, for the good of the people!"

Instantly the youth sitting around the table quickly

turn to their laptops lying in front of them. Cracking their computers open, they swiftly start hitting the keys, typing articles. The rules are established. Jack watches all of them typing as he once did. Their truths were to be soon viewed by the thousands stretching into the millions. People would now be informed of the *right* decision. Jack watched over the youths typing in front of him, realizing he was in charge now. The truth was going to come to the surface, and he was the one to unleash it. The same pride that washed over him at the protest came over him right there in that conference room. He felt as though he was some angel of justice sent down to deliver the truth to the world. In this case, honor came in the form of journalism.

SIX MONTHS LATER

Jack had kept his role as the arbiter of truth, watching over the headlines that went out. Each headline-making sure Gavin Bishop stayed in the golden spotlight while Javier was dragged through the mud, whether it was true or not, for *good* reason. Slowly the people of the state began forming teams supporting Bishop or Valénica. It seemed the numbers of support double for each of them every day. Each group religiously devoted—the state splitting in two. All this as the protest continued to rage, sometimes truly peaceful, other times erupting into violent chaos.

More buildings and neighborhoods burned into ash, taking innocent lives in both of the senses. Depending on the tribe they had belonged to, people were either beaten or executed in the street, sometimes both. Statues that had been in place since the last century were being pulled down by protestors in the name of justice, though some had thought they were doing nothing more but erasing history. Jack had been doing all right for himself; his promotion had him staying more at the office than on the ground. He drifted through the city in his new sports car, trying to show it off to anybody left on the street. Jack finally upgraded out that matchbox, moving into a luxurious apartment downtown near his office, though Jack still drove to work. He spent most nights on the balcony; he liked looking down at the twinkling city beneath him. He'd remember staring up at the bright lights in the town from a distance; now, he was one of them. The days to the governor's election were coming to a close; soon, there would be a winner. However, the tension was always rising, questioning if people would see an elected candidate take the ticket.

12

Jack stands in the conference room with his team of youths surrounding him. They type and scroll through their phones, confidently feeding Jack the news. Now maskless. A flat television hanging on the wall behind Jack plays SNN, featuring their stories on Valénica. He has now become the operator of a functioning machine pumping stories after stories, always having millions of viewers click on their articles. Jack leans back in his comfortable chair, satisfied.

"All right, Zoey, talk to me; what do you got?" asks Jack.

Zoey pulls away from scrolling through her phone, turning to Jack. "I'm going forward with the Russian scandal; it's an article linking Russian agents supporting Valénica's campaign."

"What's the title?"

"I don't have one yet, maybe, In Bed with Russians?"

"Scratch that. Make it, From Russia with Love: How to win an election. I want a full breakdown of the Russia story. Got it?"

"Yes," replies Zoey as she turns back to her phone, continuing to scroll.

"Okay, Julius, my man, what have you been working on?"

Julius stops typing, looking to Jack, "Right now, I'm just about to publish a story on his taxes; I went ahead and linked it to some failed investment properties he'd been tied in. I don't quite have all the tax information, but I think that raises a few alarms as it is."

"Good, I like it. It'll get people talking. We just need buzz! Keep up the good work." Then Jack turns his sites on Holly, "Holly, what do you got?"

Turning away from her computer, she says, "I've been doing a story on Bishop, how he has plans to help the state once he's reelected. One of the issues I've focused on was homeless; I figured a lot of the people have some opinion on that. It just goes into raising taxes for a cleanup team and special housing."

"Oh yeah, can't walk through the street without stepping in someone's shit or piss. Good work, keep covering Bishop; we want to seem diverse in our product."

Jack doesn't say anything but nods over to Zack, who is ready for him.

"I've just been compiling some of his interviews to get his opinion on some of the social programs. He's been putting down healthcare a lot; I know when people read Holly's article, they're going to get riled up because they'll see Bishop trying to help people and Valénica- well not helping.", Zacks says.

"That's good work, making it cycle back to one of our stories; I like it. It looks like you all are keeping up the good work. Make sure to hit social media with this. I've been looking at the numbers, and we've nearly tripled our viewership, so that means something we're doing is right."

They all laugh.

"All right, I'm going to head out for a bit; I'll let you know if I come back. If I don't finish the work, you got here before you go home, of course."

Jack gets up from his seat, walking out of the conference room to the elevator.

Sitting behind the wheel of his sleek car, Jack zips through the streets of downtown going towards the mountains. While at a stop sign, Jack sits with the top down, taking in the sunlight. His eyes wander off; next to him in the street, he sees an older couple, both grey-haired and crying, their business closed behind them—more victims of the lockdowns. A slither of remorse runs through Jack as he stares at them, then he notices above the couple stands underneath a billboard promoting Javier. Quickly Jack whips out his phone, snapping a picture of the couple crying underneath the billboard, leaving out the business. Jack looks back at the picture, their bodies covering the permanent closed sign hanging over the front door of what was once their livelihood. Jack smirks as he sends the picture to his team with the text message reading: *Someone use this picture in an article!* The light turns green. Jack turns his eyes back to the road, pressing on the gas pedal. He continues driving towards the mountains with the wind brushing his face.

Driving through the charming homes that hang off the edge of cliffs, Jack now felt a part of it. He once looked at the affluent houses in mystery, as though there were secrets behind their doors. Now Jack was in on the hush-hush. The same overly prideful smirk stays on his face as he quickly loops around the winding streets going up. He pulled up to Gavin's home; the front gates sealed. Jack looked over to the miserable gate attendant in the right corner. He casually threw up his hand towards the attendant, who pressed a button opening the gates. As soon as they swung open enough, Jack dashed through. He quickly passed through the road surrounded by tall trees, finally pulling up to the driveway.

Jack parked, got out, walked towards the front door, noticing a car. It was menacing, a foreign silver Bugatti Divo, which sat asleep in the driveway. Jack couldn't take his eyes off the gallant car. Just then, the front door opens; Gavin is walking out a man, he looks a couple of years younger. His wired beard hides a weak chin, greased hair pulled back into a queer ponytail, and he looked fragile like a twig.

"Thank you for helping me out during this time. It means a lot. Don't even worry about that thing; consider it taken care of.", Gavin says, winking at the man.

The two shake hands and nod. The stranger turns to look at Jack; they make eye contact. His pale, sunken eyes hid an ill empty desire. His face is familiar, but Jack can't put a name. He just watches the stranger slide into the Bugatti; within seconds, he races down the road out of sight. Jack turns to Gavin.

"A friend?" Jack asks.
"Yeah, you can say that. Just one of those big tech virgins. Come inside, please."

Jack walks inside as Gavin holds the door open for him.

The two of them gather in Gavin's study. The room is sophisticated, with dark oak walls surrounding numerous books stacked on top of each other and cultured oil paintings hanging above them. Jack takes a seat in a short yet comfortable leather chair. He turns to a cigar box sitting next to him on a nearby table. Opening the box, he takes a cigar putting it to his mouth, lighting it. Gavin fixes Jack a scotch on the rocks, passing it to him. They both sit across from each other, enjoying cigars and hard whiskey.

"I have to say, thank you for the press coverage. The polls have been looking great.", says Gavin letting out a thick cloud of smoke from his mouth.

"No problem, what friends are for. You aren't in the slightest worried about the polls though, aren't they just guessing games at this point?"

"Worried?" Gavin laughs, ripping another cloud, "Why should I be worried?"

"I mean, they're almost neck and neck with you just barely peeking out. That means something isn't working or could be better. Maybe I'll look into digging up some new stories."

"Oh Jack, don't you know anything about politics. Look, I'm not worried, because being neck and neck like this is normal. The more important thing is that I'm leading in the polls. If I wasn't, I'd probably be pulling out my hair right about now. I'm not, in any case. Instead, I'm here enjoying a drink with my friend."

"I suppose you have a point. Those uh, virgins, they help you feel better about the polls?"

"Just because I don't like to worry myself doesn't mean I don't like security either. No, those tech boys are helping me, you know, with information and everything- its a pro-quo situation. You understand?"

"Yeah, of course."

"Listen, Jack; I got a favor to ask."

"What's going on?"

"I haven't seen anything new with these scandals about Valénica, nothing new coming to light about taxes or anything of that matter. It's been a bit slow. Unless you might know something, I don't?"

"No, my team and I haven't found anything either. At least nothing hard-hitting. You know I'm starting to think it's all a hoax or something."

Gavin chuckles, "Right. Anyway, I've meant to ask, would you consider going down to the pits, so to speak?"

"What do you mean like what I used to do?"

"Yeah, or have you got comfortable behind that desk."

"I'm still young enough to roll in the mud. What'd you   need?"
"I need someone to infiltrate one of his rallies; maybe you'll get something good there. It's perfect, nobody there will know who you are, except for you and me. You might get some real hitting stuff from him. You've seen how he acts on t.v."

"In that case, I can get somebody from the team to do it."

"No. I know it seems menial, but I want someone that I trust out there. Not to say I don't trust your team, but you know, you and me, Jack, we've known each other for a while. You know how it is."

"Well, okay. I'll head down to one of Javier's rallies."

"Good, there's one tonight; it's going to be at Lake Hollywood Park. Eight o'clock."

"All right, I'll be there. You know, I've always wondered how it is that people feel comfortable going to one of those rallies, all pressed up against each other. It's like they forgot there was a virus going around."

"Yeah, that virus. Sure is a bore not being able to do anything lately, but it's all for the protection of the people."

"I'll drink to that."

The pair clink their glasses before throwing the rest

57

down their throat.

13

Hoards of people walk towards the Park, trying to find a spot to stand and sit among thousands of people circling a stage. The people there are dressed in vibrant reds, they wave miniature flags, and their cars tattooed with bumper stickers. They anticipate Javier walking out on the stage, like some rockstar. Jack stands in the crowd, ready with his camera, just like the old days. Already he doesn't feel comfortable in this particular crowd of people; he has his guard up. Then music plays, getting people excited. It works as they begin to cheer, jumping up and down. The spotlights come on, a figure emerges out of the shadows stepping into the light. Javier runs down the stage with a broad smile; he waves to his people, the crowd breaks out into roars. They stretch their arms up towards him; he throws back buttons with his last name printed on the front. Javier dawns his signature deep navy blue suit with a striped bright red power tie. Taking a moment to gather himself, Javier moves behind the podium in the middle of the stage. He looks back at the smiling faces staring at him, waiting for him to speak.

He starts, "I know this year has been a tough year for

many of you, and I thank you with all my heart for being able to make it out here tonight. I know some fears, lies as I like to call them about this virus, keeping some people from coming. That's okay; all the support counts. I must say though; I am loving the energy out here, that's all thanks to all of you, thank you!" Javier claps, the crowd cheers louder "Seeing all your faces here I'm reminded that there is still strength during this dark time, that people are willing to come together even when rapid fears are being let loose. Solidarity is important during a time like this. Which is why I plan to make sure the people of this state come first! I want to bring more jobs back, make it more affordable, so we don't have people racing out of the state, and I want to clean the streets!"

The crowd gives thunderous applause. Jack, sitting on a thick tree branch, captures photos. He takes in Javier's words. A small voice in the back of his head dismissing his words as lies. Yet Jack can't help but actually be captivated. Javier speaks with bombastic vocabulary, but not nearly as bad as he led himself to believe. The more Jack listens, the further a little wall in his head begins to crumble slowly. Some of the stories he's written seem spineless, the work of his team weak. He finds himself more in a state of shock as Javier continues to speak.

"I was driving through the city just the other day; some parts are disgusting; by the way, I was passing by one of the more poor parts. I called this young man over; I asked him why he was living in a box on the side of the road. Do you know what he said? He said because this state is getting too expensive, straight out of the college

59

with a degree, he ends up homeless, just tragic. That's under Bishop, not me. I want to help the kids of tomorrow have a future waiting for them. Bishop doesn't care about that. Do you know what he cares about? Making deals with those monsters at big tech!"

Suddenly a little bubble of anger balloons in Jack; he keeps listening.

"This state is so beautiful and popular, but I'm looking at the numbers of residents, and it just keeps falling. Bishop has failed this state so that people are taking off in record numbers, and I want to fix that. I want to bring back everything that made this state so attractive. You know it, I know it. Look at the streets; they're disgusting; we need to clean up our beloved home. These protests, they're not protests, let's be honest. They destroyed and brought havoc to your lives, and I want to bring law and order. We need to reopen businesses. We need to protect each other, not destroy each other. We need to make California great again!"

The crowd cries with applause. Everyone rises to their feet, clapping, smiling, tearing up. American flags wave through the air. Javier smiles, taking in all the approval. Fireworks shoot up into the sky, bursting into colorful sparks glowing in the night sky. The cheering continues, even reaching new volumes as the music begins to come back on. Jack, suspended in disbelief, lays against the tree. The wall, which lay in his mind broken, but not destroyed. He takes another photo before climbing down the tree. An ounce of reality was running through him, questioning everything he had believed. He gathered the images of heroes and villains in his mind separating them between a fine line, but the line seemed strangely blurred.

He tries snapping out this confused state as he moves through the enthusiastic crowd. He stops in front of a child in the middle of the excitement. His thick mask nearly covers the small child's pudgy face, but Jack can still look into his deep brown eyes. He couldn't be any older than five years old. They stop, staring at each other for a moment. The child reaches in his pocket, taking out a button with the name *Valénica* printed on the front. With the button in hand, the child stretches his arm towards Jack. He doesn't know how to respond; he's completely taken back. It was as though the simple act of kindness had been lost until that moment. Oddly it seems foreign to Jack, but he accepts the pin, gently plucking it from the child's hand. The pair stare at each other, Jack's heart is suddenly filled with warmth; no longer can he think of lines, but only decency. The child is then lifted in the air by his father, having him sit on his shoulders. Jack continues to move through the crowd, still hailing loudly. His mind feels separated from him; it's as though he can envision himself shuffling through the hoards of people circling him.

Then he hears a familiar voice call out his name. The voice is sweet yet loud enough that it echoes through the crowd. Maybe he was going crazy. The voice calls out his name again and again. Jack stops; he looks around, trying to find the source. Jack's eyes widen, and his jaw nearly drops as he watches Lisa come out of the crowd moving towards him while calling out his name. Everything suddenly seems like a sequence from out of a dream, random. Jack almost doesn't recognize her dressed more casually, yet her beauty sets her apart from everything else. She smiles as she walks up to Jack; he smiles back. He can feel the excitement weighing down his chest.

"Jack!" exclaims Lisa as she quickly goes in for a hug. Jack hugs her back.

"Hey!"

"Just when I thought we'd never meet again, here we are!" Lisa says, she looks down at the camera hanging around Jack's neck. "What are you doing here?"

"Oh-I'm just covering the rally. I didn't know you were a supporter."

"Yeah, I am. Listen, I want you to meet my boyfriend."

"Boyfriend?"

The word instantly sends shocks through Jack's mind; daggers plunge into his heart, the single phrase bulldozes and shatters any love-filled illusions. Then a broad smile stretches across Lisa's face before she lets out an amused laugh.

"I'm kidding! Oh, Jack, you're so sweet. Why don't you take me out."

Jack chuckles, "Yeah, all right; let's go."

Together the two walk arm in arm away from the crowd.

With few restaurants opened, they were all set up the same way; the pair sat right outside a cafe on the sidewalk. A chocolate shake sits in front of Lisa while

Jack has a coffee. They are close to the cars that run up and down the street, blasting their engines. Their motors echoed through the streets for everyone's displeasure. Jack and Lisa didn't mind; it felt like it was just the two of them. However, every other engine passing through nearly proved them wrong.

"So, you've been doing quite well for yourself these past couple of months. Judging by the new car."

"What? New car, I've always had that car."

"Oh, I'm sure. It must have been at the shop that day at the party, or else you wouldn't have gotten a lift there."

"All right, you caught me."

"You want to know how else I can tell?"

"How?"

"You have that little spark, I don't know how to explain it, but you can always tell when a person is doing good. It's like they have a light around them that attracts people. I know I might sound crazy, but the point is I'm glad you're doing good."

"I don't think you're crazy. I know exactly what you mean. I saw that when I first saw you." Lisa smiles as she blushes, "Anyway, thank you, I've been hustling since the last time we met. What about you, how's life treating you?"

"Oh, I've been fine, just working on the campaign trail is all."

"Wow, so you're actually one of the hardcore supporters, uh?"

"I don't know about hardcore; I mean, we've got some people who are willing to go above and beyond, but me personally. I'd just like to help, is all."

63

"I'm guessing you approve of your candidate then?"

"Well, obviously, I'm guessing by your tone, you don't."

"I'm not his biggest fan."

"That's okay; some people aren't. He's not a perfect man. He's flawed, but who isn't? It's just important that I like him. I guess that's one of the benefits of living in a country like this."

"What's that?"

"We can both be wrong.", replies Lisa with a charming smile.

"Yeah"

"Say, you're not one of those crazies, are you?"

"Crazies?"

"Yeah, the type of running around bullying people, smashing their homes, and burning buildings down? Those are the crazy ones. I feel sorry for them sometimes."

"Oh yeah, why is that?"

"I look at all the videos and sometimes ask, why would people be so devoted to something so destructive. I think they're some of the loneliest and lost people."

"You think so?"

"I mean, they claim they're doing that in the name of justice, but they just end up hurting other people, and they don't even realize it. Only the people who need the most love and care are willing to do that, just to belong. If that means committing something they don't believe in, they'll do it. Everyone just wants to be understood and fit in somewhere."

"Even you?"

"Even me. Except I'd rather fit in with those people who stay away from it all."

Jack reflects on the protests, the destruction, and the savagery he witnessed. It haunts him. The smell of raging fire. His heart beating with fear. The massive fights ending in pools of blood. Ringing in his ear, the amplified screams, all calling for death or help. The confusion in the middle of insanity, making him dizzy. Secretly whispering deals with angels in exchange for his life as he raced to the balconies. It never left him.

"I don't want to talk politics anymore. It's such a bore. I want to ask you a loaded question.", Lisa asks.

"Go for it."

"Did you make it?"

Jack chuckles, "I mean, maybe, I don't know. I got a nice car, a better apartment, maybe I can show it to you tonight?"

Lisa smirks, "We'll see. I mean, it seems like you got everything you talked about. I'd thought maybe you'd feel some kind of peace."

"I don't know, I mean, sometimes I feel it, but that's mainly when I'm driving."

"I see you picked up a friendly habit."

"Yeah."

"You like it?"

"Yeah, it's a good time."

"Why don't you show me how fast that new car of yours goes."

"Is that a challenge?"

"It very much is."

"All right then, let's hop in."

"After you."

Jack is behind the wheel, Lisa sits in the passenger, the top is down, and the engine roars. Jack zips out of the streets, going towards the curving hills ahead. They feel the cool air as the car scales through the mountains, going higher. Jack has his eyes on the road, his right hand on the wheel, as his left hand begins to move on Lisa's bare leg. She feels the palm of his hand caress her upper leg; she smirks. Her smirk transforms into a smile; then she leans over into Jack's ear. He can feel her soft lips just graze the skin of his ear. Her soft, warm mint breath runs across the side of his face. Jack glances as Lisa slowly reaching towards Jack's waist. He keeps his eyes back on the road. Then he feels her hand press down against his knee, adding pressure to the pedal. The tough engine blares as the speedometer moves higher. The car continues to loop around the hills, quickly passing the lavished homes. Jack is in total command of the wheel. He keeps his hand on Lisa's thigh; she doesn't mind. He glances at her; the wind carefully blows her hair. Even in the night, an incredibly soft light reflects off her, making her glow.

Soon they go as far up as they can. Jack parks his car on a small cliff overlooking the city. The bright lights twinkle in the distance. The moon shines full and bright in the night sky—the stars gleaming in the dark above. Lisa rests her head on Jack's shoulder as they stare at the view. There's a mutual sweet silence between them. Instinctively their hands slowly move closer towards each other until they're locked together. There is nothing, except for the two of them, preserving the moment. Time feels at a standstill, and all the woes of today cease.

"You don't wear a mask a lot, do you?"

"Not really.

"Why?"

"Besides the virus that may not be as deadly as people think, I don't see the point."

"What do you mean?"

"People wear masks because they're afraid. Afraid of what is to come for all of us eventually. They just don't realize that people live with it every day, everywhere they go, at every second they live."

Silence falls over them once again as they continue to look ahead. Lisa's words echo through Jack's head.

"If anything, right now, people should live. Live as if it were their last days."

Jack turns to face Lisa, "Go out on your terms?" he slowly leans into her.

"It's how you get the most out of life." she leans into him.

They close their eyes. Their lips lock together in a tender yet passionate kiss. Jack feels her soft pillowy lips cushion his own; he moves his hand up gently, holding the back of her head. Her hand presses on his hard chest, sliding up, holding his shoulder. Their yearning grows into a demanding lust. Jack's hands begin to run down, dropping to Lisa's waist. With a firm grasp, he pulls her in closer. He moves another hand gently back up towards her chest, massaging her breast. Her hand slips through the buttons of his shirt, popping it open, feeling his tight bare chest. Lisa's other hand shifts below his waist, cradling his crotch. His hand slips through her tight cardigan, now feeling her naked breast with the palm of his hand. Lisa's lips quiver as she feels a tingle run up and down her spine a s Jack squeezes her breast. His lips slide to her cheek, trailing down her neck. Her hand on his crotch, swiftly stroking him. He kisses a little harder, ripping open her cardigan; his lips move further south. Her other hand is holding onto his back, sinking her nails into his skin. His lips smacking against her chest until he suckles on her strawberry tit.

Suddenly Lisa pulls his lips away; they don't move their hands. They breathe heavily, yearning for their lips to touch as they continue to rub each other. Their foreheads touch, they look at each other with devilish smiles. Lisa gently brings her hands off Jack and places them on his, gently grabbing them to the center of each other. The pair both chuckle, their lips just inches away, they stare into each other's eyes. Jack looks into Lisa's deep emerald eyes, getting lost in the thick of them.

"I want you to come to my house tomorrow.", says Lisa.
"Sure."
They smile at each other.

14

Jack walks through his apartment with his phone to his ear as he goes into his closet. Turning on the lights, a row of suits and jackets hang.

"Yeah, I got the footage; I've already sent it to my team; they'll know what to do with it.", says Jack as he slips on one of his many sports jackets. "Don't worry; I have faith in them. They'll know what to do. All right. Goodbye."

Jack ends his call, then slips his phone into his pocket. Walking to the door, he gathers his car keys before walking out.

Jack, behind the wheel, races through the city streets, he drives towards the countryside. On the road, he finds himself immersed in fields. On each side, rows beyond rows of fields, growing vegetables and fruits. The pickers have their baskets in hand as they stand, hunch, and kneel to gather nature's bounties. The air seems cooler, fresher.

Further on the road, Jack, with the top down, can feel the little water droplets in the air. He can smell the saltwater nearby. He's hardly past anything but unscathed nature, maybe a few rest stops and gas stations, but it all seems very secluded. There's a sort of tranquility that hangs over the area, making the isolation feel like a mirage. He continues driving.

Finally, Jack reaches his destination; he slowly pulls up to a sign reading: *Lazy R Ranch*. Just adjacent to the sign is a continuing dirt road. Jack passes the sign going down. He soon pulls up to a somewhat large house surrounded by acres of green land, trees, and mountains in the distance. Jack marvels at the sight of the peaceful home. He parks near the front. Stepping out of his car, he can't take his eyes off the beautiful landscape. Lisa burst out of the house, practically sprinting towards Jack; she leaps into his arms before giving him a peck on the lips. Lisa takes Jack by the hand, giving him a tour. They walk around the property, Jack admiring it all. The grass, just slightly overgrown. Healthy trees scattered stretching to the great mountains in the distance. A barn to the side, looking as though it sat there for hundred years, adding legitimacy. Short trees growing lemons, oranges, and grapes fenced off—the fresh breeze brushing against them. Being lost in nature was foreign to Jack, but he embraced it as he did the cool air.

Tired, they rest on some furniture set outside. Birds fly over their heads, high in the sky, and sing to each other as Jack and Lisa lay comfortably on a woven couch. Jack looks at Lisa's bare feet, noticing her souls are soaked in the dirt, sprinkled with bits of grass. She stares at him with her wide smile and bewitching emerald eyes. With his deep brown eyes, he stares back.

"You know I just realized something.", says Lisa.
"What's that?"
"We barely know each other, apart from our names."
"I like to think we know a little bit more than that, but okay, what would you like to know?"
"What do you do?"
"I'm a journalist."
"Really? I hope you're the real kind. That must be exciting, always getting the latest scoop on everything. I bet it never gets boring."
Jack chuckles, "Yeah, the job can be a little fast-paced, but nothing I can't handle. So, what is it that you do?"
"Nothing exciting like that. I'm still in school, or if you can even call it that anymore since everything's gone online, it just feels like a total sham to keep going."
"That sucks. I mean, I wish I could relate. To be honest, I never went."

"You never went?"

"Nope. After high school, I just didn't really see the point. All I wanted to do was cover stories and deliver the truth. So, that's what I did, saved up some cash, then started going where all the stories were and just filmed and wrote articles."

"That's amazing!"

"What are you learning at school?"

"I'm not even sure. I can't decide on a major. Sometimes I think it's ridiculous you have to pay some money then jump through some hoops for a little piece of paper that says you're able to do something. I mean, don't get me wrong, I get it-you have some experience and a little credibility. But if I knew what I wanted to do, I'd just do it. And try to be the best."

"I mean, there must be something you're passionate about."

"I guess I dabble in writing."

"Dabble?"

"All right, I guess you can say I do more than dabble. I've written a book-it's just poetry though, nothing like a story."

"So, you're a writer. Why don't you put your work out there?"

"If we're honest, I don't think I'm that good."

"That's what they all say. Let me hear one."

Lisa doesn't answer but looks at Jack with a playful smile. She plays with the idea of revealing her writings to him. She isn't sure yet; they're too personal. Maybe sometime in the future, but not now.

"No, I'm too shy now."

71

"What come on, just one."

"Maybe some other time. Besides, that'll be too easy of a way to get to know me. We just have to see where this goes."

"All right then, one day.", Jack winks, "You have a nice home. How do you manage it?"

"What do you mean?"

"Yeah, you must have a good job to afford a place like this. It's beautiful."

"Oh," Lisa chuckles, "This is my family's home. I'm a writer, remember? If it weren't for them, I'd probably be in a cheap motel, broke with just a book of poems."

Jack chuckles. He turns his head, gazing at the green grass, the established house, and the scattered trees. Everything looks natural; it's peaceful, undisturbed from the chaos of the city life. He begins to understand Lisa a little better now. Maybe being left alone in a place like wasn't so bad. Calmer than the noisy city, where people were losing their minds.

"Are they here?"

"I don't know, to be honest. I think one of my sisters. We all have crazy schedules."

"Should I say hello?"

"It's not a good time right now. It's not that they don't like meeting new people, but they're all just super busy working right now. So, everybody is a bit on edge."

"Okay, well, would you like to go for one of those drives?"

"I'd like that."

They jump into Jack's car, speeding off. Jack presses

down on the pedal letting the engine scream. The wind splashes through them as they continue flying down the road towards the beach. Soon the mountains look drier, the fields on the sidelines turn into tall rocks and piles of sand. The air is chilled, the smell of the salty sea becoming potent. Jack pulls up into a small deserted plot. He parks his car next to the sand, along the side of the road. The waves run up and down the shore. Still barefoot, Lisa races Jack to the beach. He rushes after her while taking off his shoes. Jack comes running behind Lisa, grabbing her, trapping her in an embracive hug. They laugh before running into the cold water. Jack, with his pants, rolled up, barely stands in the water.

Lisa stands deeper in the water, the bottom of her sundress becoming soaked. Lisa teases Jack before pulling him towards her in the deep end. He hesitates before following her. Instantly Jack regrets it as the icy water splashes his warm skin. He doesn't care by the time he's reunited in her arms. Lisa laughs as she splashes Jack water; he splashes her back. Back and forth, they continue to throw water at each other. They rush into their arms, look into each other's eyes, their hands slowly wrap around each other. The sun beaming in the background, and the waves crashing against them. They lean closer to each other, passionately locking lips. Smiling and holding hands, they walk back onto the shore; the warm sand grabs onto their soaking flesh. Together they retreat onto a rock; sitting on it, they let the sun dry them while they watch the sun steadily fall into the ocean. They hold each other tight in their arms, Lisa laying her head on Jack's shoulder.

Watching the sunset, Jack realizes nothing outside of this moment matters. He could care less about the raging protest burning cities, the political feuds breaking out; it all seems like a distant blur. It was all trivial bullshit that he had been wrapped up in, along with the countless masses. His daily routine is surrounded by news footage of this and that, then overblown reactions. It all seemed pointless and stupid. Then he thought back to that day he signed the papers for Dan; maybe he'd gone too far. He wondered if he had not been driven by his desire to be something, would he have met Lisa. He felt her soft fingers brush gently through his hair. It was a soothing feeling. Maybe there was a point wrapped in the bullshit. Perhaps it wasn't for nothing. Everybody just wants to find happiness. Jack thought people have been looking for pleasure in the wrong places. They had been looking to the wrong people to deliver their contentment. People forgot how to live. They wanted things the easy way now. Foolishly, they thought happiness was a vote away. They were propelled too deep in fear to break out and find any real joy for themselves. Jack and Lisa continued to keep each other close in their arms, staring at the sunset.

Coming back to the ranch, they went back to where the furniture was. They sat underneath some trees. Strung above were little lights that glowed as dusk approached—Jack, sitting on a couch with his arm over Lisa and her head lying on his chest. Jack felt that peace; Lisa once talked about; it was here, at that moment with her. Just then, they hear footsteps behind them in the distance coming closer. Before they could see who it was, the stranger already made it to them. Javier Valéncia, dressed in a navy vest, loosened tie, and matching slacks, came out the back door.

Javier smokes from his Sherlock pipe, draping him

74

in a thick fog of smoke. He stares down at Jack, who still has his arm around Lisa. Instantly Jack is starstruck; he could feel his jaw hanging from his mouth. Javier looks intimidating up close; there were brutality and wisdom in his eyes. He continued to puff out smoke. Jack couldn't believe it; the coincidence was too much. Someone had to be fucking with him. Javier then extends out his arm towards Jack.

"I don't think we've met before, Javier Valénica.", Javier says before biting down back on his pipe.

Jack sits frozen, but quickly he jumps to his feet shaking Javier's hand. He tries to understand what the hell is going on; at the same time, he scatters getting his thoughts together.

"J-Jack Parker, nice to meet you.", says Jack, totally nervous.
"Lisa, why didn't you tell me we were going to have guests. I love to meet new voters.", Javier says, winking at Jack before bursting out of laughter.
"Sorry, I didn't think anybody was going to be home. I thought you'd still be out campaigning."
"Yeah, well, we were making good on time, so we finished up early and just got home. Everyone's inside after a long day. Hopefully, we made a difference."
"I'm sure you did; they go crazy for you. How was the rally?"
"Oh, it was fine. To tell you the truth, I'm a little weary. I think I'm going to head inside and rest up a little. Hey, you kids want something to eat?"

Lisa looks towards Jack, who still stares at Javier both surprised, yet amazed. Examining Jack's expression, Javier is amused, chuckling a bit. Lisa giggles, turning back to her father.

"I think we're good, thanks."

"Okay, well, if you need anything, the staff will be here for a little longer."

"Thanks."

Javier walks back into the house. A trail of smoke follows him, still smoking out of his pipe. Jack's eyes are wide, and his mouth still open.

"You know if you leave your face like that, it's going to get stuck.", says Lisa as she sits comfortably back down on the couch. Jack joins her.

"Javier Valéncia, is your father?" asks Jack.

"Yeah, that's right."

"I don't get it; you two look nothing alike; you don't even look like his wife.", says Jack, still bamboozled. Lisa smirks and giggles more.

"Yeah, that's right too. What about it?"

"I'm sorry, I'm just trying to wrap my head around this."

"You know, had I mentioned you were a journalist, he would've probably greeted you with the barrel of his gun."

Jack's further eyes widen; Lisa laughs.

"Oh, loosen up, Jack, I was kidding!" Lisa replies, continuing to laugh.

"So, how are you two related?"

"We're not."

"Well-what the hell is going on? I feel like I'm solving a damn riddle."

Lisa chuckles, "Okay, well, if you must know, I'm adopted."

The lights turn on in Jack's head. He gets the picture.

"Ohhh, that makes sense. So, you're not a Valénica, that makes sense now."

"I'm an honorary Valénica. I'm honestly pretty lucky."

"What happened? I mean, if you don't mind me asking?"

"It's a bit of a long story; you really want to hear about it?"

"I'm a journalist, remember; I got to get the scoop."

"Well, I never knew my actual father, if you can even call him that. The son of bitch ran out on my mother and me. Though I don't remember much about her either, she died when I was five. Then after that, I ended up in the system bouncing from foster home to home. I was at school with Javier's daughter, Layla; we grew up quite close. I guess I grew on them, and they took me in not long after."

"Oh my god.", Jack replies in amazement. "That's incredible."

Lisa smiles, "That's what I tell myself too. The rich real estate mogul who took in the sweet orphan with a heart of gold makes it sound like it's from one of those princess movies."

"Yeah, no kidding."

"Listen, Jack, promise me you'll keep everything

from today a secret. There are so many lies that come out about my dad. He's already under enough strain from the campaign. He doesn't need anything else surprising him. Just please keep all this between you and me."

"For you, I promise."

"You're sweet, Jack, thank you."

Lisa kisses Jack. Even a soft yet warm kiss can't distract him from the bombshell truth he just saw unfold. He then gently holds her hand, kissing the back of it. They smile at each other, their eyes revealing a growing fever for one another. The pair return to comfortably laying on the couch, snuggling close. Though Jack's mind still blown away, he can't be going crazy too early in life. He tries to forget everything, except her; he holds her closer.

15

Jack sits at the head of the table in the conference room; his youth team type and scroll away on their phones writing propaganda. Concentrating, Jack's eyes move around the room. He watches his team put out hit pieces after hit pieces on Javier. Their articles only praise Bishop and honor the protest that eats away at cities. Javier rushes to his mind, but more importantly, Lisa. Jack can't stand the feeling of hurting her. He didn't know her father, apart from the smears he frequently publishes, but he questions his judgment. His integrity feels remote. Suddenly Julius and Holly walk over to Jack with a laptop in hand; they set it down in front of him.

"All right, boss, check this out; Holly and I edited the footage you gave us. Tell us what you think.", says Julius before playing the video.

A clip from Javier's rally plays, "I was driving through the city just the other day, some parts are disgusting, by the way. I mean just look at the streets, they're disgusting." another clip plays, "These disgusting protests destroy our lives."

Smiling, Julius and Holly look at Jack, who is still sitting in silence.

"So, what'd you think?", asks Holly anticipating approval.

Jack doesn't know what to think anymore. He thinks of Lisa; his thoughts amplify. All the smears hit him all at once. *"Valéncia bad"* rings in his head over and over again. People were skimming through their feed, believing all his lies and half-truths. Suddenly, he feels something invisible weigh him down. *"Valéncia bad,"* again rings through his head. The dozens, thousands, millions, of people, purposely shielded from the truth. He might as well have been brainwashing them to think whatever he wanted. He could have told them ice cream was terrible because Javier ate it, and sales would have plummeted. People were walking around blind, further diving into the reality Jack had created for them. They were asleep in their fortified bubbles. Jack could feel the pressure increasing. He felt trapped; it was an intense suffocation. Terrified, Jack could feel his sanity begin to slip. He quickly jumps to his feet.

"It's good! I'll be right back.", says Jack as he dashes out the doors of the conference room.

"My article on the protests just got eighty-thousand views!" exclaims Zoey gleefully; Zack high fives her.

Jack walks to the end of the office, bursting into the bathroom. Turning on the sink, he splashes the cold water on his face a couple of times. Jack grabs a few paper towels. He stares in the mirror as he wipes off his face. It's as though Jack doesn't recognize himself anymore; the young rebel is gone. He was now a shell of his former self. Jack wasn't a writer or journalist fighting for justice. He had been a fool, writing what was acceptable. Hardly a rebel, more of a sell-out.

Coming out of the bathroom, he slowly returned to the conference room. Just as Jack was about to walk in, something came over him. He stood in silence, watching his team sit around the table working. They were all in deep concentration, continuing to write out smears and delude viewers with hoaxes. A nauseating feeling crept up on Jack as he kept looking. Carefully he began backing away, further and further, until reaching the elevator. He got in; the doors closed, it went down.

Sitting on the couch in his luxurious apartment Jack watches the television. Bishop is giving one of his speeches, wooing the crowd with his charm.

On the wide television, Bishop says, "You know I've heard some of the vulgar things my opponent has said about this fine state, and it breaks my heart. He drives around this city, our great city, and claims it, along with its good people, are disgusting. I can't help but think that my opponent has a heart full of bitterness. I think we have different philosophies toward life. Personally, I like to see the potential in what things can become. With time and given care, one can flourish, which is an important quality in leadership. My opponent would like to highlight the bad things and twist them turning them ugly. I see the good, I see the beauty, and I wouldn't trade it in for anything else in the world. To live in this beautiful state, well, it's just such a privilege. So many people come from different walks of life just to be here, well I can't help, but feel some semblance of pride when I think about that..."

Jack lowers the volume. Standing up, he walks to the window staring down from his grand view. Watching the few cars run up and down the street, the even fewer people walking on the sidewalk. Looking up, he admires the majestic architecture of the skyscrapers, the beautifully crafted apartments around him. Jack turns around, observing the elegance in his lavished apartment. The marble fireplace, the sleek tall white walks, the expensive furniture, the new wide flat television, and the spacious polished floors. It definitely wasn't the run down sardine can apartment. It was better; It made him feel like nobility. Though in that worn-down apartment, there were times he felt that same way when he wrote something true, or at least he thought it was. Even though the drywall had been peeling, the wooden floors were creaking, and the only view was a scampish alley filled with rouges alike. Then reflecting on those small victories, he didn't feel like nobility. He felt the emptiness surround him.

Suddenly, there's a knock on the door. Not expecting any company, Jack cautiously walks over. He cracks it open, able to peek outside. Javier, with two other men, stand in the hallway. Jack's heart instantly sinks to the bottom of his stomach.

"May I come inside, please? I would like to talk.", asks Javier calmly.

Jack, with hesitation, replies, "Sure." he opens the door.

Only Javier walks inside; the two men accompanying him stay out front. He looks dapper as he always does, dawning a slick dark charcoal suit and red power tie. Javier looks around Jack's apartment, impressed. Jack watches Javier move toward the window; he looks down from the fantastic view.

"Impressive place you got here, Jack.", says Javier turning back to Jack.

"Thanks. Uh-can I get you anything?"

"I'm fine. Thank you."

"What about your friends outside?"

"They're fine."

"Should I be worried?"

Javier laughs, "Oh Jack, just because I'm Mexican doesn't mean we're all some cartel, boss."

"Oh, I'm sorry I didn-"

"I know, I'm just busting your chops, relax. Come on, let's have a seat; I want to talk."

Jack sits on his comfortable couch while Javier sits across from him in a possibly more comfortable chair. Javier reaches for his infamous Sherlock pipe; right before he lights match, he quickly looks to Jack, "Do you mind?", "No." Jack quickly responds. Javier continues to light the match, puffing away. He doesn't say anything right away but just stares at Jack. He can feel Javier's eyes examining him. Javier reaches back into his jacket, pulling out his phone; he scrolls through it before turning the screen towards Jack. It's an old picture. Javier stands beside his beautiful wife, standing in front of them, their two children, and Lisa. The photo seemed ancient, Jack noticing everyone's youth, mostly Javier's once raven black hair and the braces glued onto Lisa's smile.

"That's me, that's my wife, Maria, my oldest daughter, Bianca, my second oldest, Layla, and of course my youngest daughter, Lisa. This was about a year after we adopted her. This was also the year she started calling me her dad and Maria, mom. We were beyond happy; my heart nearly burst. I remember adopting her; what a nightmare fueled paperwork that was. Really it was a bitch, but I'd do it again and again for her. I know she isn't my own flesh and blood, but I'd take a bullet for her all the same. I'd do anything for her, including protecting her from anything malicious. Are you malicious, Jack?"

Jack is thrown for a curve, "What? No, I'd never do anything to hurt Lisa!"

"I never forget a name, Jack Parker. Did you know with one quick search on somebody, you can pretty much find out anything about them? I mean, that's how I found your address. Though tell me, I don't think you did before, but what is it that you do?"

"I'm a journalist."

"Is that what you told Lisa? Or did you tell her you were a journalist for SNN? The same news company that

83

deliberately prints lies about me by the hour."

A chill runs through Jack; he feels caught as Javier darts his eyes at him. Javier slightly separates his lips, letting a coil of smoke run out his mouth. Jack can feel Javier's eyes sink deeper into him.

"I've been honest with you, Jack, so now I want you to be honest with me. Are you using my daughter to get to me?" Javier leans in, "Because if you are, I will cave in your skull right here, right now, and I could care less about my campaign, I'll throw it all away."

Jack swallows nothing as Javier refuses to break eye contact. Javier sits there with the pipe in his mouth empty-handed, but it's as though Jack can imagine a gun pointed right to his head. He can feel the nose just press against his skull.

"Sir, Mr. Valénica, I am not using your daughter. I care about her very much. I do. I can promise you that!"
"For your own sake, I hope you're telling the truth. I'm a very wealthy man, which makes me a powerful man, and I can promise you, I will do anything to keep my children happy."
"I believe you. I know it's hard to trust what I say, but I'd like for you to know that whether you believe me or not, I would never do anything to hurt Lisa; she is very important to me."

The leather chair squeaks as Javier leans back, still smoking. He looks at the window, off into the distance. He chuckles a moment later.

"Look at that view. You probably paid a fortune just for that, uh?... You know, I grew up poor. I remember playing in the front yard with a stick and my imagination. I remember the neighborhood junkie passing by every afternoon. He was friendly enough, probably on his way to get his next fix. As I got older I knew I couldn't stay there anymore. My parents had done the best they could with what little they had, but I knew I had to do better. My first job was at this fast food place", Javier chuckles, "I had forged some documents so I could work early, to get an extra buck or two. I worked my way through college-junior college, earning a degree. Then I went into real estate and made something for myself. I never forgot the gutter I was forged from. Did you know they have the lowest school attendance?"

"Where you grew up?"

"I've made many donations there over time, I've done what I can for myself, but now I want to give back to my community. Sometimes I think that's why I took a shine to Lisa because she reminded me of myself. I love her as though she was my own. I'll always think of her as that little girl with the halo. I treat all my kids the same by pushing them to do better than me for their own sake. I won't always be around, so they'll be left to their own devices one day. I think that's why everyone's against me because I want to challenge people to do something. To find meaning in a meaningless existence rather than being."

Silence drapes over both Javier and Jack. Javier lost in his thoughts, letting more smoke out from his mouth like a dragon. Javier then rises to his feet; he walks towards the door. Jack follows him. Turning the knob about to walk out, Javier turns to face Jack.

"Jack, I don't want to upset her but, if you have any respect for Lisa, you'd tell her the truth, not just her, but everyone.", says Javier looking Jack square in the eye before walking out.

Jack is left speechless; the only thing he feels is the guilt that spreads through his body like a virus. Jack walks over to the fridge picking out a scotch bottle, then pours it into a glass. He throws the bitter-tasting scotch down his throat in hopes of curing some of his guilt. It doesn't. So he tries another shot. He feels the pressure trapping him again. To hell with the shots, he drinks from the bottle, nearly ripping it empty. The confined force is washed away, but the guilt amplifies. Jack continues to drink from the bottle. Knocking himself out would be better than to feel the anguish smothering him.

16

Somewhere in a neighborhood with deep cracks in the sidewalks, sharp metal gates surrounding old homes, cars rotting on bricks, there is a loud fight on display. Neighbors silently watch from the safety of their screen doors, a young couple arguing. A young woman, in tears, stands in her front yard. She is afraid to go near the young man, who looks slightly older than her. He stands by the driver's side of his car, about to take off.

"DO I LOOK LIKE I GIVE A FUCK? BITCH GET THE FUCK BACK INSIDE THE DAMN HOUSE!" yells out the young man.

Just then, the sound of children crying echoes from

the backseat. The young woman can feel her children's pain; she cries helplessly.

"Please! DON'T DO THIS! GIVE ME MY KIDS!" pleads the woman as streams run down her cheeks.
"FUCK YOU BITCH!" replies the man.

The woman throws her crying face into her palms, peaking to the side—a police car making the evening patrol curses through the street. Quickly the woman jumps up and down, waving her arms at the car, desperate for its attention. The vehicle instantly pulls over, a young cop in uniform comes out. His eyes directly look at the woman.

"PLEASE HELP! HE'S GOT MY KIDS!" pleads the woman, sniffing through her tears.

The young officer turns his focus on the young man, still standing by his car. The officer starts to approach him carefully.

"Step away from the car.", orders the officer.
"Man, this ain't got nothing to do with you.", replies the young man confidently.

The officer slowly moves his hand near the grip of his gun. He keeps it there. Suddenly the two children cry louder from the backseat. The man doesn't seem scared but annoyed. Neighbors cautiously emerge from behind their screen doors, gathering to their front yards. The officer's eyes glance at the kids wailing before setting his sights back on the man, who becomes more frustrated.

87

Still, the officer steadily walks towards him.

"Man, this has nothing to do with you! Get the fuck on!" says the man.

"Look, just calm down, step away from the vehicle."

"Man, fuck you pig-ass-motherfucker! Do something!"

"Step away from the vehicle NOW!"

"This ain't nothing to do with you! Get the fuck on!"

"This is the last time I'm going to warn you."

"Count this one as my last time to bitch!"

The young man begins reaching behind his back. The officer stops moving, quickly clutching the grip of his gun.

"STOP MOVING, PUT YOUR HANDS UP!" warns the officer.

The man keeps moving his hands behind his back, cautiously reaching for something. The cop's heart races so fast he can hear the beat echo in his head. The man's arm is still for a moment before it starts moving again, this time from out behind his back.

"STOP MOVING!"

The young man starts to slide his arm up. The officer intensely focuses on the young man's arm. He's nervous; between them, it's anyone's move—the critical moment of exchanging blows. The pressure is melting away at the young officer. Suddenly, CRACK! A single bullet cuts through the young man's torso sending him to the cracked pavement. He's still alive, twitching in a pool of his blood; laying beside him is a sharp pocket knife. The officer, with his gun, lowered, moves towards the man. The young woman races from her yard to the car, instantly reaching for her two children. Gathering them in her arms, comforting them as tears crawl down their soft pudgy faces. The young officer looks at the kids in remorse for a moment. He then speaks into the radio hanging off his shoulder, calling in for a medic.

17

Hundreds of people under the shade of night march in city streets, dawning black, holding signs reading: *Justice Now*, *ACAB* (All Cops Are Bad), *Fuck Cops*, *Dirty Pigs*, *Colored Trans Rights*, *Hands up don't Shoot*, and infamously, *No justice NO Peace*. Their sequenced stomps echo through the boarded-up streets. Their furious chants are like the blaring of ominous trumpets. Some hold makeshift shields made from garbage lids, some carry airsoft guns, and others contain an arsenal of suspicious cans tied to them. Shops lined up and down the streets have their windows and doors boarded up with thin walls of wood. The wood planks read: *We Support You*, in graffiti, as though it were the blood of a lamb on their doors. Some shop owners stayed behind, standing ready with their guns to protect their life's work. Signs with intimidating black fists wave in the air. Fireworks are shot from the menacing crowd landing on the ground near the boarded-up shops. The ones who stayed behind carefully watch the mob. With enough insults, enough threats, and dares, sprinkled with idiocracy, a clash soon breaks out. Molotov's fly in the air, crashing into the windows of business, torching them. Trying to save their community, the ones who stayed fight the angry mob.

Cars speed out of control amid a chaotic battle crashing into buildings, hitting people. Brawls break out in the street, throwing fists, tackling each other, charging at each other with no hesitation—anger screeches, like a war cry ready to die in battle. A frail older man, scared by the hell surrounding him, stands in front of his locked up bar. Soon a gang of angry people dressed in black surrounds him. One of them throws a punch; the older man isn't ready to get knocked down; he keeps his stance. Another fist is thrown at him, followed by another, then a third, finally sending him to the hard pavement. Together the gang begins stomping on the older man cracking his delicate bones. Blood seeps from his face. The group continues to stomp on the old man shouting, "Fucking Racist!". A young man runs towards the small gang, yelling, "Dad!". The son tries to fight off the group but is outnumbered. Soon his friends arrive as a backup, trying to help.

One of the owners who stayed behind runs around with a fire extinguisher towards the blossoming flames. Quickly he blasts foam, desperately trying to keep the city from turning into ash. Suddenly, he is knocked to the ground when two rage-filled protestors repeatedly punch him on the side of his head.

It has become the people and their willingness to survive. The people left abandoned, their police and firemen told to stand down. Blood splatters on the ground as people beat each other like savages. All the rules deserted; nothing matters but the rain from the flames of hell. Soon tall fires eat away at the buildings creating an inescapable wall of a broiling inferno. A fog of thick black smoke looms over the night sky, blocking any view of the full moon or stars. Then new untouched cars parked in rows in a dealership lot is set on fire, causing a booming explosion.

Above the chaos, laying on his couch, Jack sleeps but is suddenly woken up by the deafening explosion. Everything is still fuzzy from the boos as Jack rubs his head. Slowly he gets up, accidentally kicking over the empty bottle of scotch on its side. He doesn't pay any attention moving towards the window. Jack looks down, the boozy haze clouding his head disappears. Instead of the mesmerizing view he paid for, it's blocked by a thick cloud of smoke, with fire stretching out. He hears the screams, the fights, the madness from his tower. They're too loud to ignore. He watches people he once walked along with, in the name for good, on a warpath of revenge. The veil was lifted; behind it was nothing but insanity. An irrational, paranoia-fueled rage, he created, now unleashed like a wild dog off its leash. He can't stand by and watch. Jack turns around, quickly leaping to his front door.

Coming out onto the street Jack immerses himself in the depths of anarchy. A runaway car with people barely hanging off the side windows nearly cuts him down; he hasn't even left the sidewalk. Without hesitation, Jack sprints into the thick of it, looking for somebody, anybody in need of help. Looking around, he doesn't know who needs help or who is aiding in destruction. Everything is grey, hidden beneath the ash-filled air. Out of nowhere, an angry young scrawny man dawning black throws a punch right in Jack's face. Jack backs away, trying to look, who threw the blow, but before he can even open his eyes, another punch meets his face. Jack starts swinging his fist into the air, hitting the young man. Jack's got him; he repeatedly strikes, each one harder than the last. Soon Jack finds himself hovering over a foolish young man dressed in black, bleeding from his nose and mouth. His nose shifted to its side with bone sticking out and teeth missing, all soaked in blood.

Just as he is about to smash his knuckles into the young man's cracked nose, he stops himself. He slowly rises to his feet, then looks at his blood coated hand. He's disgusted as blood runs from his fingertips; he looks down at the young man with his face nearly caved in, now remorseful. Jack backs away, trying not to add fuel to the fire. Moments pass before he witnesses another young man holding a rifle as an angry older man looks ready to pounce on him. The young man's eyes are focused on the wild man, who wobbles like a caged fighter trying to find the perfect time to strike. The young man keeps a tight grip on his rifle. Jack is the only one who seems to notice this defying moment. It all seems slow to Jack, as though the world stopped turning for him to witness this one act.

Just then, the older man pounces off the ground leaping towards the young man with the rifle. The older man tightly grabs onto the young man's rifle. The young man keeps a tight grip, trying to shake him off. "NOOO!" yells out, Jack watching it all unfold. BANG! The older man falls to the ground bleeding; the young man looks over him in disbelief. Quickly Jack dashes to them; he raises his hands as he comes near the young man with the rifle. The young man looking at Jack's empty hands, lets him go towards him; Jack immediately goes to the man bleeding out on the pavement. He quickly looks towards the young man, still staring in awe. Jack can hear the stillness of time in his voice as he yells, "What are you doing? Call 911!" to the young man.

"They won't come!" replies the armed young man. "Fucking protestors!"

Time kicks back in as Jack starts to tend to the bleeding wound. He's never done this before; he doesn't know the first thing to do. Then a gang of people dressed in black begins to walk over to the young man. Jack doesn't pay any attention to them; he quickly takes off his shirt, swiftly wrapping it around the man's bleeding torso. The gang closes in on the young man, who backs away with his rifle aimed at them. They all completely ignore Jack, who throws the dying man's body onto his back. Jack struggles to move, but he has to. He rushes to the nearest hospital, thankfully not too far. As Jack walks through what looks like a chaotic nightmare, he barely hears the man breathe. The gang ignores the dying man but focuses only on the young man, swarming him. They could care less who dies for the cause; they just need martyrs.

"STAY WITH ME!" yells Jack as he continues to carry the dying man.

The weight hits Jack causing him to collapse. He drops the bleeding man onto the ground. Jack jumps to his feet in pain, picking the man back up, barely slinging him over his back. Soon Jack is draped in blood. Sweat rains down Jack's face as he scrabbles to get the dying man to medical attention.

93

"Help...I need HELP!" calls out Jack to no one, as everyone else is in the mix of madness.

Jack continues to walk, finally with the hospital in his sights. Jack pushes himself, knowing he'll be there soon. Jack trips, making both of them hit the ground. Quickly Jack picks himself up; with his knees weak, he finds strength lifting the dying man. As he reaches the hospital, his body gives out; he now has to drag the man with the remaining effort left in him.

Crowding the front of the hospital is an angry group of people dressed in black, threatening the wounded and the medic's who dare help anyone. Jack doesn't care anymore; with the little strength he has left, he elbows his way through the crowd, barely holding onto the almost dead man. Jack lifts the man again, holding onto him as tight as possible, as he tries to make it through the hospital doors. The line of cops keeping the crowd from going into the hospital notice Jack, tired and slathered in blood. They quickly reach for him, pulling him in. Suddenly, someone from the mob grabs onto the dying man's leg.

"LET GO! LET GO OF HIM!" Jack yells at the crowd.

One of the cops smacks the hand from the crowd with his baton. The mob moves in on the cop, sucking him into their anger. They quickly beat him, distracting them from Jack, who moves through the line of cops with ease. Jack's grip is tight on the dying man as they collapse on the hospital floor. Quickly nurses and doctors rush to their aid."Help him...please.", says Jack weakly as he lets go of the man, giving him to the doctors. The bleeding man, who barely breathes, is thrown onto a gurney quickly rushed into the halls. A nurse helps Jack back to his feet. He looks down at his bare chest, painted in rich ruby red blood. Then two officers rush in; they drag in their fallen brother, who suffered from a gunshot wound, leaving his arm hanging by a thread. His veins dangle out; a cracked bone lightly swings with his lower arm. The officer screams to the top of his lungs in agony. Jack nearly vomits, seeing the wound. The officers help their brother, who probably wishes for death compared to a long-burning torment. The nurse ditches Jack for the officer, leaving him to fall back into a chair in the corner. He turns over his palms, bathed in blood, tears begin to build up in Jack's eyes. The voices around him are angry, vengeful, and suffering,

Dawn. Jacks walks back into his apartment, painted in blood, covered in bruises, draped in scares. He looks around his lavished apartment. Suddenly he erupts in anger throwing anything in his sights against the wall, destroying his own life as he destroyed many. The expensive home, the fast car, the fine clothes were meaningless. It was stained with his sins.

Jack's apartment was now a mess; he sat among the broken glass and overturned furniture. He could see smoke float into the air from his glamorous view. He walks to the window pressing his forehead onto the glass, looking down at the destruction beneath. All the meaningless death. The unnecessary destruction of his own doing. He watches people scrabble in the ashes, desperately trying to put their lives together. Ash comes

95

down from the sky, like snow draping the streets in a bleak grey. The sun begins to peek out from the smoke-filled clouds.

The door opens, Jack turns. The sunlight beams down on Lisa as she walks into the apartment. She looks around at the mess, but her eyes stay on Jack, disheveled. He's coated in dry blood and covered in bruises. She's speechless at the sight of him. Jack slowly walks to her; she's frozen in shock. Jack opens his arms, hugging her before Lisa can wrap her hands around him. He bursts into uncontrollable tears. He slides to his knees, crying into her stomach. "I'm sorry, I'm so sorry.", Jack says, weeping into the seams of Lisa's baby blue dress. Lisa, unsure of what to do, gently pets him on the head. She then kneels, wrapping her arms around him. Lisa coddles him in her arms, gently stroking him with one arm as he continues to sob. She gives him a peck on the forehead. At the window, smoke flies into the air, taking her attention. She closes her eyes while continuing to hold Jack, now broken.

18

Jack lays down in his bed, now clean with all the blood and ash washed away. Lisa walks into the room, opening the curtains, letting the sunlight through the window. The sun's rays are bright enough to wake up Jack. His eyes slowly open, he slides up as Lisa sits next to him on the bed. She wraps her arms around him.

"What the hell happened last night?"

Jack doesn't answer yet. He could still feel the warm blood on his bareback and the crushing weight of the man. Then the image of the cop with his arm barely attached to his body. He can still hear the sound of fires raging, explosions booming, and terrified screams. Jack turns away from Lisa, sitting on the side of his bed. He rises, going to the window. He leans against his wall peering down the view. The streets below him in tatters, business in ashes, and cleaning crews trying to sort through the rubble. Some people drop to their knees in anguish; their lives burned into nothing. The guilt and shame start to close in on Jack finally. He could no longer escape from it. He looks back at Lisa; cluelessly, she looks back at him, concerned.

"Nothing good. It was a nightmare come to life.", replies Jack, almost coldly.

"Whose blood were you covered in?"

"I don't know, some man. He got shot. A lot of people did. I did my best and carried him to the hospital, but I don't know if he made it."

"I'm sure you did everything you could. I was watching someone streaming what was going on last night. I realized you were near it; I'm just glad you're okay."

Lisa walks over to Jack wrapping her arms around him; she lays her head on his chest. He can feel her soft hair brush against his skin. Right as Jack is about to lay his hand gently on the back of her head, Jack stops himself. Pulling back his hand, he looks away from Lisa. He carefully pulls her off him. Lisa looks confused; Jack holds her hands delicately in his palms, looking her in her deep green eyes.

"Lisa, there's something I have to tell you. I haven't been honest with you." Lisa begins to worry, "I work for SNN. I green-light the hit pieces on your dad; I make up lies that cause people to hate each other, I hype up Bishop because that's all I'm allowed to do. I'm sorry. I never met to hurt you or your dad. I never meant for any of this to happen. I just wanted to be somebody. I'm sorry, I never meant to hurt you."

Backing away, Lisa stands in shock. Jack waits for her to say something, but she can barely look at him. Jack steps closer; she steps away.

"I care about you, Lisa, and I'm done lying. I want to be free."

With tears building in her eyes, Lisa replies coldly, "Well, consider yourself completely free!"

"Lisa…" says Jack as he goes to her. She's already heading towards the front door. Before Jack can say another word, she's slammed the door, gone.

Jack, frustrated, leans his head against the door. Just then, a vibration comes from his pocket. Jack takes out his phone, not even looking at the caller.

"Hello?" Jack says miserably.

"Hey Jack, how the hell are you?" asks Gavin, pumped with enthusiasm.

"Oh, you know, just hanging in there."

"Right, that's cool. Listen, I'm having a little garden party at my house tomorrow, you should drop by. It's nothing big, just one of the fundraisers before the debate."

"I don't know…"

"Oh, come on, I'm sure you can write a fantastic article about it," Gavin laughs, "What'd you say?"

Just as Jack is about to turn down Gavin, suddenly, an idea pops in his head. "You know what, yeah I'll drop by; what time?"

"Great! It starts at four. Remember nothing but my good side, okay?" Gavin laughs again, "All right, see you then, pal!"

Gavin hangs up. Jack has a plan.

19

Jack speeds behind the wheel of his slick car. He scales the mountain lined with lavished mansions, along the way to Bishop's grandiose home. Jack rushes through the already opened gate. His engine roars through the air as he drifts into the front, parking his car. Stepping out, Jack dawns a classic dark plaid grey suit with a black tie and his hair carefully combed, making him look like a real executive. He walks towards the backyard.

The backyard is set up elegantly with a green manicured grass, lights stringed above, and wine at every other table. The same crowd as before, powerful all scattered, enjoying themselves. They're dressed very formally, most in dark colors. There is a thin podium with a microphone set up on the balcony. Standing beside it is a handsome profile picture of Gavin reading: *Fighting For California*, right below it. Jack scoffs at the blown-up image. Gavin walks over to Jack. His dark brown hair slowly turning grey is meticulously combed

99

back; he wears a deep navy suit with a wine-colored knit tie. He flashes Jack with his signature charming smile as he shakes his hand. Gavin casually wraps his arm around Jack as they walk deeper into the backyard.

"Hey Jack, long time no see, how are you doing?"

"I'm doing okay; I see you're doing good."

"Well, tell you the truth, I could be better. I just got word that Valénica is up in the polls, but those tech virgins are doing their best. At least they better be."

"Their best? What do you mean?"

"Oh, you know, trying to boost morale. You can't win unless morale is up. Oh, by the way, thanks for that favor; I read some articles and watched a few videos. Donahue was right; I knew I could count on you. Now hopefully, I can just count on your vote." Gavin laughs, "All right, Jack, enjoy the party."

Gavin pats Jack on the back before going back to mingle with his people. Wine is passed around; Jack reaches for a glass. He throws the red wine down his throat. Now Jack waits in a crowd of phonies, half truthers, and liars for the perfect time to strike. He passes the time by talking to the people there, though they all sound the same, programmed to hate Javier and love Gavin without reason.

It was all in fashion. Power was the hottest thing to possess. Jack could finally see what most of them genuinely were, the world's finest actors. They convinced the people of their cities and states, they were the most caring, intellectually gifted, and humble beings to lead them into a brighter tomorrow. In reality, if the people asked for something, politicians didn't have a clue what

100

they were talking about. They would just repeat it enough times until they got enough votes to win. They were as dumb as the rest of the world. They were out of touch, holding themselves up in their gated mansions, with round the clock security. Some people knew this and wanted to be left alone. Others refused to peek behind the curtain, choosing to stay in a choreographed world. Jack knew not all the faces that were at the fundraiser were power tripping addicts. Some worked in office to truly better society; they probably hated these things as much as he did. Those kinds were few and far between. He watched as Nancy Melosi spoke with a small group of other leading women, perhaps on her fourth class of wine. She looked shakey; her words probably slurred and stuttered as she spoke. Jack examined her fine clothes, the gleefully smile on her wrinkled face, and her carefree attitude sipping her fifth class. Then he remembered her refusal to help the people through the ongoing virus. She halts aid for them, all because of a petty fight with another colleague. Even when politicians lost, they still won. It was their people that suffered. Their suffering was driving them to insanity. It all reeked of bullshit. These people didn't realize what they had, only what they could and couldn't get away with. It was all pathetic; to them, it was all a big game. Jack was sick of it; they were getting away with too much. He was more disgusted with himself, blindly aiding them, convincing people which side was the best, deluding their minds.

Gavin finally got behind his thin podium. He looked down at the crowd smiling, charming them with his winning smile. Gavin slipped on a mask just before the camera's started rolling. The camera's made sure to

101

avoid any other people in the shot. He had stood before his flock; in anticipation, they patiently waited to hear his sermon. Jack looked at him, probably different than most in the crowd. Still, everything Gavin had built for himself was, on some level, impressive. Though it begged the question, how could a public servant be a millionaire? Gavin was a crook. People expect thieves to look like big-nosed, old, hunched over men with top hats and capes. The truth was, the best-crooked men were hard to pick out from the crowd. They needed to hide among the people, so they would think he was one of them. Once trust was gained, and they were given enough power, they could do whatever they want. In Gavin's case, it was easy for him to earn the people's trust. He was tall, handsome, practically born a winner. Jack knew now; Gavin was like the rest of them, power-hungry with a big appetite and a fatter wallet to line. Gavin looked to the cameras and started his speech.

"Thank you, those of you at home shielding yourselves from this deadly disease inflicting all of us. I would also like to give a big thank you to the people of this city for sacrificing for the greater good. I know these lockdown restrictions have been strict, but it will help us save lives, so thank you for your understanding. I want to be clear; there have been a few things said about me in the past couple of weeks that I want to clarify. I first want to explain that I love this state and want nothing more than to see it blossom. Second, I am disgusted by the low-level behavior of my opponent and his supporters. They gather in mass numbers as though unaware there is some virus roaming through our air; it is genuinely deplorable behavior..."

Jack couldn't hear much more of this; he had practically been writing Gavin's speeches. Besides, right now, it was the perfect time to strike. Everyone's attention was focused on Gavin, and Gavin was focusing on the camera's. Jack cautiously walked around the crowd going towards the side of the lavished house. He walks up to a door, slightly cracked open, probably for the staff. Going through the door, he walks through a hallway. Jack carefully tip-toed through the hall, passing by the kitchen, filled with chefs working at the grill and waitresses coming in and out. He made his way to the foyer. It was modern, designed beautifully. Though the house only stretched two stories, the ceiling was high, with a chandelier attached. Jack carefully walked towards Gavin's study.

Opening the door, Jack made it inside, still impressed. He spots what he has been looking for, Gavin's laptop, conveniently laying on the oak carved desk. Wasting no time, Jack quickly leaps at the machine. He flips it open, the screen flashes on. It's a locked page; a password is needed. Shit, maybe he didn't think this through enough. Pausing, Jack thinks for a moment. All the possible words in the English language hit him all at once. Any one of them could be the password. He can feel the clock ticking. He thinks. Something comes to mind; it sounds too stupid to be real. Fuck it; he types it in any way. Jack enters in the phrase, "*Fighting for California.*" The screen opens; he's in.

Jack begins to scroll through the computer. He searches all his files, recent searches, and photos. Nothing damning. At least not enough to wake up people. Then he searches through his emails. Clicking on

103

Gavin's inbox and drafts, he finds what he needs. Jack's eyes widen as he goes through them. Mountains of evidence of inflating virus deaths, benefiting the doctors at the hospitals. Admitting he moved the elderly and infected together, killing the old. Proposals to extend the lockdowns, permanently shutting more businesses. Deals with the tech virgins to censor Javier. Under the table deals with Ukrainian powers, and Chinese intelligence spies, honeypots. It was all there—all Gavin's dirty laundry for the taking. Jack dug into his jacket, pulling out a flash drive. Without hesitation, he sticks it into the computer, downloading everything. Jack watches the screen in complete amazement. Just minutes pass by; it's done. Jack swipes out the flash drive keeping it close in his pocket. He walks towards the door, slipping out unnoticed as he came in. Jack walks through the house, going towards the front door, impressed by his ability to do hard-hitting journalism still.

"Holy shit.", he whispers under his breath.

Just then, a voice comes behind him, "Sir, you can't be in this part of the house." jumpy Jack turns to one of the staff members.

"Oh, yeah. I was just stepping out."

The staff member follows Jack to the front door opening it for him. Jack walks out with a wide smirk on his face. With a real sense of pride, he walks to his BMW. Jack sits proudly behind the wheel, putting on a pair of cool black shades. He turns on the engine, releasing a menacing roar. Stomps on the pedal while spinning the wheel, burning tire onto the clean pavement. Then zips off of the property leaving smoke in his trial. Jack speeds down the mountain. The air splashes him as he dives down the loops going towards the streets. He casually drives one-handed with the smirk still intact on his face. The screeching of his tires echoes through the well-groomed neighborhood, leaving tracks behind. Jack bounces onto the city streets. He keeps heavy pressure on the pedal as he glides through the moving cars. Without hesitation, Jack quickly laps the cars next to him. He slides in the other lanes as he maneuvers around them. Already Jack was near his glamorous apartment. Jerking the wheel, he pulled into the garage.

He was back in his living room, sitting in front of his laptop. It all felt natural, typing away on his computer writing articles in a lonely apartment. He was finally back to his element; he relished in content. The pressure wore off. Importantly a part of his soul was coming back to him, though he knew the feeling wasn't forever. Still, he reveled in his writing. He was writing something real. Something he could finally be proud of. It would get him fired, and people would hate him. However, he wouldn't be a writer if it wasn't the truth. People hated honesty that poked and prodded at their bubbles. They would rather sit in darkness and be led like sheep. Jack couldn't take it anymore. His soul was dying. A man without a soul is nothing but a spineless sack of flesh. A blacklist would wait for him. The stillness of division unmoved.

Though at least he could offer them a way out, through the truth. A few hours passed by; it was very late at night. The articles were done. They were juicy. Sure to get Jack hated and sure to expose Gavin. He thought politicians were either the most menicale motherfuckers to ever rise to power or complete trust funded imbeciles that were voted in. Either way, there was no way the articles weren't going to get attention—the moment of truth.

Jack hesitated to hit the button to send the articles out in the world. He looked over them, again and again.; they didn't need any changing. Everything was there, the lies, the corruption, the real faces. A small part thought about not sending it, keeping them locked away in a particular file, somewhere. He thought of Lisa. He thought of the feeling of being a real journalist. Hitting the button would maybe bring her back to him. Perhaps it wouldn't. If he did send it, at least he could feel a semblance of his soul belonging to him again. That was enough for him. He quickly pressed the button. He leaned back in his chair, taking a deep breath knowing millions of people would see it by sunrise. He didn't want to think about that right now. He stood and looked around. He went to a dresser in his room, opening it, there was a ziplock bag. Inside, three rolled joints were in it. He took one out, lit it, lay in his bed, and tried to relax. His mind drifted off into numerous thoughts, which branched off into more ideas. He could already hear the crap he was going to get from Donahue in the morning. He decided to show up late, not giving a shit. If he were going to die, it would be on his terms. With his soul intact and the pressures of morality lifted, he laid on his bed smoking.

He thought about Lisa. Her soft brunette hair, with a hint of blonde. Her alluring emerald eyes. They were hypnotizing, like vortexes; anyone could get lost in them. Her soft, light skin. Her pillow-like lips. He remembers the tenderness of them, pressing against them with his own. The way they stretched into that warm smile. Her perfect curves, taking the shape of an hourglass. He
106

could feel his hand move up and down her body smoothly. Her tender and supple breast. What he missed, most of all was her spirit. It was like a cheerful glow that surrounded her and attracted others to her. Unbound and limitless. What he couldn't believe is that for a brief moment, she wanted him. She could have anyone, but she chose him. Jack didn't lack confidence. In the past, his judgment with women had always been lousy. Before Lisa, the girls he got mixed up with were shallow. They were concerned with things that didn't matter, never living in the moment. Meeting Lisa was refreshing. She was real and spontaneous, down to earth and graceful. Beautiful and intelligent. Everything he needed. The cruel realities of life were myths in her presence.

Now he was alone, left with an expensive apartment, fast car, fine clothes, and better weed. His soul now felt complete. No pressures. It was all fine. Though he was missing an essential part of what he needed now. Her. Though at least he had her, even if it was more a moment. He'd be all right. Jack continued to puff into a pungent haze.

20

It was morning. Jake woke up earlier than he expected. He wasn't even late for his job. The cruel part about it was, he wasn't sleepy. Going back to bed wasn't going to happen. He did the first thing most people did in the morning. Check his phone. Sure enough, Donahue sent him an email. For a split second, he thought about ignoring it and spending the rest of the day at the beach. However, his curiosity got the better of him. He swiped at the screen, opening it up. The screen brought him to

107

the email.

The little words in the left-hand corner read:

Parker,
Meet me at the office. 10 am SHARP.

All capitalization. Jack was going to die. Jack took a deep breath, sat up, and thanked his god that he was still alive and breathing. He went to change into his funeral attire.

The elevator doors opened on the office floor; Jack walked to his death sentence. He wore a black suit with wide peak lapels, a light grey shirt, and a black woven tie; Jack walked to suicide in style. Jack walked past the glass conference room filled with the youths printing out more lies by the hour. Jack nodded at them, but they just glared at him. He could feel their negativity dig into his chest. Jack did his best to brush it off. What did they know? Most of them never even had anything decent to write, just lies. Most of them whined and bitched to get what they wanted, never really doing the work, or taking the beatings like most people. They were misguided, part of the same generation that clung to their childhoods with a dying breathe, dumb kids.

Jack continued to Donahue's office. Or his old office since the virus made people clear out of buildings. He opened the door and walked in. Dan was watching the television, his news network while drinking coffee.

"Hello, Dan."

He ignored Jack. He just kept watching the television, so Jack watched with him. The news anchor was the same one who was paid way too much money, only to lie and bend over for corporate. His name was Jerry Lemon. He was black and gay, and in the modern world, that makes you nearly untouchable. Guilt was a strong emotion for people who gave a shit about the things that are long gone. He was going on.

"In other news, leaked emails linked to Gavin Bishop came out today from one of our reporters at SNN, though they weren't verified and are still pending further investigation...in other news, Javier Valénica still seems to be self-hating with this next story..."

Jack chuckled. Of course, they would go that route. Crowds. The worst part of it was, if there was no Javier Valénica, there was no SNN. They didn't realize it, but he was their business, even though nearly everything they reported on him was crap. People ate crap; Jack looked at the numbers himself. High viewership.

Dan stood up from his chair; he laid the coffee gently down on his desk. Jack turned to him with his back held firm.

"You think that little stunt you pulled was cute, Parker? What was that? Some sort of message, you working with Valénica now, uh?" Jack didn't answer; Dan wasn't looking for answers, "I wanted you to see that because I want you to know who runs this fucking business. You work for me; if I don't like your shit, it's nothing. You're nothing. If I decide one day I want a race war, then I'm going to get my goddam war! I decide

109

what people see and what they're allowed to think! Got it? You got any more tricks up your sleeve?"

"Maybe I do. What are you going to do about it?"

"I'm going to sue the fuck out of you, you fucking prick."

"Sue me? For what, reporting the truth? You know what, on second thought, sue me because then people will get a chance to see some actual journalism and have some faith in it again."

Dan got real close to Jack's face, but Jack kept his cool. His mind was ready to take a punch; if he took that punch, he'd throw one right back.

"You think you're so fucking funny, uh? Well, you're not going to be funny when your ass is on the street with the rest of those fucking bums out there! You had it all, Parker, you had money, a nice car, I brought you out of that shit hole of an apartment, ME! And this is how you repay me? YOU MOTHERFUCKER; YOU FUCKED ME!" Dan's voice got quiet, "Why? What was it in for you? At least tell me that."

"I was tired. I was tired of the lies. I couldn't get a good night's sleep, and last night I slept amazing. Before, I felt like I was someone at the bottom of the barrel. You and Bishop, you're nothing, even with all your money and power, you're still big pieces of shit, you know that? Did you that Dan, with all your money, your big houses, bimbos to fuck, you're still a piece of shit because there IS NOTHING REAL ABOUT WHAT YOU DO! You're all empty, and I pity you."

Dan takes a swing, and Jack dives. He's quick, back on his feet, but Dan rushes at Jack, sending him to one of

110

the leather couches. Jack didn't know what to do. Then he closed his fingers and clapped hard on Dan's ears. He sprung up, holding his ears, which were now red. Jack shifted to the side and launched his foot into Dan's stomach, sending him back.

Jack got up. He had no idea if that move would work. Not wasting another second, Jack sent his fist upward against the edge of Dan's chin. With the back of his fist, he quickly tapped Dan's exposed throat. Dan, a man of nearly fifty, couldn't keep up. He fell to his knees, holding his throat, barely able to breathe, and definitely couldn't talk. Jack had more talking to do.

"Don't you see what we're doing? People are going out there and killing each other because we keep pushing these lies. We've created teams, maybe we didn't alone, but we sure helped. Now, look at us. Our city is burning, and people's lives are being destroyed for a couple of more views. Is it worth it, Dan?"

Dan's face was red hot like he'd just eaten a spicy pepper. He was outraged, still barely able to talk. He rose to his feet, looking about, ready to snap at Jack with his sharp teeth.

"Get out...You're fired!" said Dan with a weak raspy voice.

Dan just stood there with fumes nearly coming out of his ears. Jack didn't stay longer than he needed to. He was already out the door. Just outside the office, the youths quickly gathered near. They darted their eyes at
111

Jack as he made his way to the elevator. They wanted to destroy him. They felt let down, betrayed. Not one of them followed him out. Jack knew they were fools.

"Better get out while you can. You're just digging your graves.", said Jack as he passed by.

The youths watched him get inside the elevator. The doors closed, it went down.

21

Jack laid around his apartment for the next few days. He had been doing what most of the country had been doing for months—growing restless in their own homes, waiting for the madness to die down. Though it looked like it was here to stay. People were miserable, they drank, smoked, fucked, but it wasn't joyful. It was empty. They did it out of boredom, out of desperation to feel something.

In the days since he had got fired, Donahue didn't forget or his youth team. For his crimes of honesty, the people with the media's support sentenced him to exile. Jack was put onto a list of other journalists seeking out the truth. They were all deemed liars or conspiracists; their audiences were ostracized; Jack now excommunicated from established media and their rigid supporters.

His remaining fan base now cut in half because of his leaks, yet he was a free man. Free and going broke. He looked through the internet for new places to live. It seemed like the sardine can was calling his name. He didn't care; he could have cared less. Things might have looked like they were going down, but he was going where he needed to. Once and a while, everyone needs to plummet down, so they can be real. If they stayed up for too long, they'd be stuck in their assholes without finding their way back.

One thing was for sure. Jack had time to think. Not many people used this time for that, but Jack did. He thought of his plans. He was ready to go independent. Start his own business, a little late in the game, but better late than never. He had felt chained up for too long; people told him how to write, what to write, sucking out his soul each time. Now that he was not bound to loyalty, but himself, he had an opportunity.

22

A few more days pass by. The apartment was nearly all packed up. Jack had found a place, somewhere out of the city limits. It was a little house past the canyons, resting near the mountains. He was inspired to take off where people would leave him alone. He finally understood what she meant. He was just sad he figured it out too late. The television was on in the background; he never paid much attention to it anyway. It was just background noise. Then something caught his attention, an ad for a special event—the first and only debate between Valénica and Bishop. Jack couldn't believe it, soaking up all the information. He couldn't miss it. He wanted to watch Bishop fail; the damn fool deserved it. A joke with too much power. Jack knew this only too well.

Jack continued to throw things together in a box, then tape it sealed. Suddenly, there was a knock at the

113

door. As Jack opened the door, his jaw nearly gave, Lisa stood in the doorway. She made his knees buckle, his heart race, and made him feel alive. Lisa wore a pink v-cut top, tucked into some light jeans, and nude-colored heels. Jack always admired her elegant fashion sense. She looked perfect, as she always did.

"Hello.", she said quietly.
"Hey, long time no see."
"Do you mind if I come in?"
"Sure."

Jack opened the door; she walked in. Lisa sat her purse and jacket at the counter. Her eyes locked onto the boxes stacked on each other, scattered in the apartment.

"You're moving?"
"Yeah. Looking for a change of scenery."
"Look, I'm going to get right into it. I saw everything you leaked. I just wanted to come by and say thank you. I wanted people to know my dad wasn't all bad. Certainly, not as bad as Bishop with his secret deals with Ukraine and fake death numbers."
"You inspired me. You reminded me of why I started doing this, the truth."
"Thank you. You took that leap; that's pretty brave. I guess that's why you're packing then, uh?"
"Honest people are either migrating or going extinct these days. I figured migrating was easier."

Lisa chuckles, she walks closer to Jack.

"I want to apologize for the way I left last time."

114

"Don't apologize. I was an asshole. I just couldn't see it because my head was filled with too much air."

Lisa chuckles again, "Jack, I never stopped thinking about you. After my little stunt, I wouldn't be surprised if you didn't think much of me."

"I think the world of you." Jack gently grabs Lisa's hands, then pulls her in close.

He looks deep into her emerald eyes. He was lost in them. She made him weak, but he didn't care. She was the best thing to happen to him in years. She was good for him, pushing him to be a better man.

"Come with me."

"What?"

"I'm moving out of the city, into a house, with some land. It's not much, and it's nearly two hours away, but it's something."

There's a brief pause that has Jack worried until a smile stretches across Lisa's face.

"Okay."

"Okay?"

"Yeah, I will."

The pair smile, stretching from ear to ear. Jack excitedly lifts Lisa, twirling her around before locking with her lips. They remember the touch of their lips rubbing against each other. What starts as a tender kiss turns into raw passion. Jack places his hand firmly on her bareback, pressing her up against him. With one hand, she wraps her arm around him. With another hand, she feels his hard yet smooth chest. Jack hoists Lisa into his arms, taking her into his bedroom. They ripped each other's clothes off. Under the few sheets Jack hadn't

115

packed away yet; they made passionate firey love. It was the most exciting feeling Jack had felt since he quit his job. They laid against their nude, sweaty bodies under the sheets, tired and nearly breathless. Jack looked over towards the window, staring out at the lovely view. It was already sundown. It felt like minutes had gone by, but in reality, it was hours. Lisa snuggled up to him; he laid there, keeping her close in his arms. If this was his life going down, this is where he had belonged.

Jack woke up a couple of hours later, morning, but the sun hadn't come out yet. It was early. Too early to hear his phone vibrating next to him. Barely awake and more annoyed, he swiped the screen, with his eyes slightly squinting open.

"Hello?"

"You fucking asshole!"

"Good morning to you."

"You've fucked me, you've fucked my campaign. They got the FBI on my ass now. The fucking FBI dick! All because of you. You know I'm going to name drop you, and they're going to come and arrest you!"

"Oh, Gavin, it's you. Arrest me, for what? Reporting important information to the public. I don't think the people mind all too much about you lying about how many people died from the virus and your little buddy-buddy business deals with Ukraine and the Chinese honeypot."

"FUCK YOU! Don't forget I got you where you are; I introduced you to people, I got you in when nobody else would have batted a single eye. Let's not forget who ran that little team of yours. You're a liar-a fucking liar, you've ruined yourself, pal!"

116

"Do I sound worried? No, I sound like a guy who needs more sleep. So, maybe one of those tech virgins can help you censor the truth; you're all good at that. And for your information, I might've been a liar, but I came clean, pal, and I feel amazing."

"You've ruined everything I built, all of it! If you think I'm going to forget about this, you got another thing coming, you understand?"

"Yeah? Blow me."

Jack hangs up the phone. Completely unfazed, he slides it back on his dresser. Now Jack can continue with his sleep. He snuggles back close to Lisa, shutting his eyes.

23

Moving day. The last of the boxes are packed up in Jack's sports car. The lavish apartment, still nice looking, was now a shell. It was ready for the next person— someone who likes to live in an expensive cubical. Jack stands in the middle of the room, getting a last look at the place. Somewhere deep inside, he would miss everything, the fantastic views, the space, the proud feeling of owning something glamorous. Lisa came behind him, wrapping her arms around him. He held her, pecking at the back of her hands. He's ready to move on, looking out the window; the sun already started coming down. Jack had hoped to be on the road by now since the new place is pretty far and isolated. He would probably be driving in the pitch black. He might as well get used to it.

"Are you sure you don't want to go to the debates tonight? Your dad would probably like the support."

"No, it's fine. My sisters are going to be there. He didn't mind if I missed the debates. He just said that I better be there for his victory lap when he's sworn in."

"He's that sure?"

"He's a hundred percent sure."

"Speaking of which, he was sure about you moving in with me?"

"I mean, I told my parents about it, but I'm also an adult, Jack." Lisa chuckles.

"Yeah, but I mean on account of what I-"

"At the end of the day, you did the right thing; you told the truth. You did it knowing your boss would fire you and half of your fanbase wouldn't forgive you. It takes a certain type of person to stand up for his own beliefs even when all the cards are against him. Especially now, because people hate *you*."

"Thank you. I'll take note of that."

"Don't beat yourself up about it. Everybody makes mistakes. We just need to redeem ourselves."

"Oh, does that mean you've made a few mistakes?"

"Well, wouldn't you like to get the scoop?"

The pair playfully smile. Lisa gives Jack a peck on the lips. He wraps his hands around her waist as they walk towards the front door.

Minutes before the debate begins, the two rivals, Javier and Gavin, stand feet apart on stage. With intensity in their eyes, they glare at each other. Gavin, more so. Javier knows he's weak; he's got a lot of ammunition to crush Gavin. This debate would be the first and last time he could convince people to vote for him. He would have thought it was a no brainer for people, but they're divided by a fine line. Living in a world filled with more sheep in bubbles than people.

Javier wore a classic navy suit with a robust striped power tie. Gavin also wore navy, almost black, with a deep wine red colored tie. They both looked put together and ready to kill each other. Just outside the building, supporters of Javier rally waving around flags and holding banners with smiles. Little did they know another wave of supporters were coming, the ones they weren't expecting. Few cops stood on the sidelines, wearing heavy armor. There were a lot less of them. Nearly half fired, easier than solving a problem. They were terrible for Gavin's reelection, so he cut them loose.

Jack sat behind the wheel of his sports car. Lisa sat next to him. The rest of the boxes, packed in the trunk. They drove through the city with the top down. Going through the streets, they noticed it was starting to get packed. Traffic was picking up. No doubt because of the debate. Suddenly, Jack had a gut instinct; he could feel an ominous presence hang over him. He kept driving in silence but stayed on alert. Lisa spun the radio dial, listening in on the debates.

The debates were beginning; Javier felt ready putting on his charismatic smile. Gavin displayed his charming smile as the camera's started to roll. Introductions were made. The candidates waved; there was hardly any applause from a barely existing audience. The mediator began with the first question.

"My first question to the both of you is, what is your response going forward tackling the virus? Both of you have two minutes, Mr. Valénica; you go first."

"Thank you; it's a pleasure to be here this evening. I do have a plan to fight this virus moving forward. That plan consists of transparency, meaning not lying about the number of deaths by the actual virus-like my opponent", Javier gestures to Gavin, "I would allow businesses to reopen while encouraging the safety regulations recommended by the medical association."

"You'd be willing to risk lives over a few more dollars.", Gavin interjects.

Javier smirks, "The cure can not be worse than the disease. Gavin, you look at the streets and tell me there aren't people dying. This city is already the leader in homelessness; I don't think we need to further contribute to it."

In the car, Lisa smiles, having heard her father's comeback. Jack could imagine the disdain look on Gavin's face. It brought him a little comfort. Just then, Jack notices something in the rear mirror. It's a black SUV that's been behind them for too long. Jack kicks a turn, the car follows. Jack makes another turn; the car stays on his tail. Lisa doesn't seem to notice yet. Not wanting to scare her, Jack keeps his cool and continues to drive. The SUV stays behind them.

Outside the debate building, Javier's supporters cheer on as they watch the war of words from their phones. Excitement runs through them as Javier comes after Gavin. Moments later, they hear marching in the distance. Hundreds of faint voices becoming clear. Hundreds dawning black and makeshift military gear walk towards the building. The cops begin to move in.

They form a line around Javier's supporters. The menacing mass group of people shouts, "HEY HO, THAT FASCIST HAS TO GO!", fascist meaning Valénica, "A GOOD COP IS A DEAD COP!", and of course, their favorite, "NO JUSTICE NO PEACE!"

In the sky, the sun is near setting. Two ideologies stand opposite of each other in the street. One willing to go to the extremes to win. The others ready to defend themselves. In between, stand a thin line trying to keep order. The crowd of menacing young men and women continue to chant and shout to the top of their lungs. Some of Javier's supporters laugh at them. Soon the threatening crowd begins to hurl slurs, insults, anything to make the other side want to strike.

They shout, "NIGGER!" to the black man wearing a Valénica hat.
They scream, "YOU FUCKING FASCIST!" to the single mom wanting a better life.
They yell, "DIE PIG!" to the young cop, who just wants to protect people.

On the debate stage, they continue to answer questions, somewhat. They've moved onto a couple of topics, landing on different points running with them. Some won, some lost, but they keep going at it.

"Well, I think it's fair to say my opponent doesn't care about the minorities in this state. He seems only concerned with himself. Even though he is Mexican, he doesn't seem keen on aiding immigration policy. I plan on aiding anybody willing to work hard to become a part

121

of this great state, this beautiful nation!"

"That's funny Gavin, you know there's a phrase for people like you. Ever heard of the great white hope? Face it; you're just another closeted racist who thinks because he's white, you have a responsibility to people, who in your eyes, are lesser."

"I don't think that! I've done more for the minority communities   than-"
"Listen! I've employed many Hispanics during my many years in the real estate business, giving them opportunities, blacks too. That means paying them money to bring to their families. Frankly, I'll give an opportunity to anyone who wants one. Just as long as they've earned it?

"Oh yeah, what's earning it mean? As long as they vote for you?"

Gavin smirks. Javier brushes it off.

Outside, the crowd is growing restless. There is an overwhelming intensity in the air fueled by rage and animosity, ready to strike. The police brace themselves as the menacing crowd begins to crave violence; the mob is turning desperate, throwing pieces of trash at the other side.

Back on the debate stage, it's the old stale topic, race.

"Mr. Valénica, while on the topic of race, there have been killings of unarmed colored men; what is your response to the threat of people of color by police hands?"

122

"Well, I think the loss of any life is sad. But you have to understand some of these officers are walking into unknown situations. I looked over the most recent case, and the man who was shot was not only brandishing a knife-a weapon, but he was in some domestic dispute. He was not doing what he was instructed to do. Instead, he thought he could take on the officer. What do people expect the officer to do when someone with a knife is not backing down?"

"Typical heartless and irresponsible language encouraging your supporters to enact violence. I think a defunding of resources of our police is necessary. They're supposed to be our finest; we are supposed to trust them to act in the law's best interest for society's benefit. They certainly aren't acting like it. If they can not handle that type of power and trust, then resources should be directed elsewhere."

"I don't think that makes sense. Wouldn't you want more funding so police are better trained? Have you been in rough neighborhoods? *Oh*, that's right, you spend your time held up in your mansion. Let me tell you this; I come from a down and out neighborhood. You wouldn't imagine the type of domestic and gang violence that unfortunately breeds in those communities. Police should be better trained. Power must be checked."

"You're a callous man. Power in the wrong hands is dangerous for everybody. If they can not handle that type of responsibility, then it should be revoked."

Jack continues to drive. The SUV, still on their tail. Lisa has no idea; she's intensely focused, listening to the debate on the radio.

123

The crowd outside the debate building is heating up. Eyes are on the lookout for the smallest excuse to clash. Then opportunity strikes. One of Javier's supporters, branding one of his bright red hats, begins to walk towards the police line. He's alone. The menacing crowd narrows in on him. The single Javier supporter carefully goes around the police line at the very end. He gets onto the empty sidewalk, trying to ditch the coming danger. It feels like the end of a time bomb about to go off. The crowd swarms the supporter. The ticks suddenly closing in. The supporter gets lost in the menacing crowd, with just his hat visible. Swiftly a single gunshot is fired, the brains of the Javier supporter shot into the air. Instantly the threatening mob runs into the group full of supporters. The police try to hold them back, but they're outnumbered. Gas is popped, flowing through the air— multiple gun's fires, echoing through the city. The fires rise. Hell has unleashed itself.

On the stage, Javier and Gavin continue to debate. Gavin speaks, "For this state to thrive, we need transparency, honesty, and empathy. I've been backing the people since my first day in office. I will fight for them -" suddenly he's interrupted by a muffled explosion, outside. Immediately heads turn towards the front door. Security quickly barricades the doors. The sporadic gunshots from the outside are loud as fireworks. The debate audience panics, jumping out of their seats; Gavin's security comes behind him, escorting him to safety. His eyes are locked on the front doors, wondering if they will come for his head. Javier takes command, taking center stage, trying to calm everybody down.

Outside, rows of parked cars are being lit on fire, triggering explosions. People from the threatening crowd fight Javier's supporters, going for their throats. The supporters fight back. The police try to break up the brawls. They swing their batons into the air, trying to strike submission into the mania. People from all factions fire their guns at one another. Bullets mow down people, cutting right through them. Molotov's are thrown into buildings, people inside or not, they burn. Flames eat up structures, swallowing them in boiling heat. Some revel in the madness. People burst from out of the boarded shops with televisions, gaming systems, money, and jewelry in their hands. Exotic run away cars speed through the street, killing others on impact. A young man dressed in black makeshift military gear stands on top of a car, holding a flamethrower. Like a dragon, he roars, spitting fire from his gun. Soon blood decorates the city.

Clouds of smoke float into the air, the flames engulf the city in an inferno. The shade of night barely peaks through a dimly lit orange sky.

Jack still drives, now trying to lose the car behind him. Lisa continues to listen to the radio until the muffled explosions play over the broadcast. Suddenly, the radio hits dead air. Out of nowhere, a fire truck, accompanied by a swat van, brushes beside Jack, rushing ahead. For a moment, Jack's confused. In the next moment, his eyes lock onto the orange sky with flames dancing beneath it. Quickly, he jerks the wheel, spinning the car around. Lisa sees the SUV following them, going down a street; Jack makes a sharp corner. He's made some space between him and the other car. Keeping both hands on the wheel, Jack stomps on the pedal, trying to outrun the SUV, gaining speed behind them. Lisa grips the car handles. There are more people on the street than cars. They're infected with the lunacy, bringing destruction with them. Jack swerves out of the way, trying not to hit people hopping in the street. The SUV tries to avoid being slowed down. Jack turns another sharp corner. The SUV's tires scream as he drifts, making the same turn. Up ahead, a thin line of police officers march through the streets in heavy gear. Jack's heart nearly sinks as he swiftly spins the wheel. He speeds up. The SUV follows.

An anger-fueled mob of people dawning black rampage through the streets ahead, Jack slams his foot on the brake while spinning the wheel. The car wheel's screeching echo. The SUV didn't brake in time, crashing into the mob of people. They swarm it like ants, ripping it apart. Jack turns his head, watching the SUV drown in a sea of people.

Suddenly, "WATCH OUT!" Lisa yells.

Jack looks in front; a flaming van slowly rolls through the middle of the street. With only a few feet to spare, he hits the brake and turns the wheel. The sports car spins in a circle before slapping against the side of the fiery van. Crashing leaves the pair woozy; soon, both feel the searing heat and smoke slithering into their noses. Quickly, he takes Lisa's hand as he leaps out of the car. They stumble away from the sports car as fire drips inside. Within moments the flames consume Jack's car. The pair watch for a second as their only means of escape explodes. Holding hands, the two-run towards the police line. They stay close together. Out of nowhere, a pickup truck speeds through the police line. Lisa is horrified as it splits an officer in half, and another bounces off the windshield. Blood spills in the air.

"DON'T STOP! KEEP RUNNING!" yells Jack.

Running, Lisa briefly watches a police officer drag his fellow brother, whose right leg is torn off. Bullet's fly towards the police, knocking them to the ground. The police fire back. Jack and Lisa duck their heads, one officer slams his fist on the back of a rioter's head. One rioter swings a right hook towards an officer. A canister is thrown into the air, crashing down on the ground. Just moments before it goes off, Jack sees it.

"COVER!"Jack warns Lisa.

Before Lisa can react, Jack already shields her with his body, wrapping his arms around her. Meanwhile, Jack lifts his shirt covering the bottom half of his face. He shuts his eyes closed as the gas pops out into the air. Jack opens his eyes; he realizes it's not tear gas. It's a smoke grenade. Quickly he unwraps Lisa's face, keeping a tight grip on her hand, they run. Jack tries to navigate out of the insanity. The gas created a fog too thick for Jack to see through. He can't tell where he is anymore. Everything is barely visible; Jack keeps Lisa close to him. He turns his head, watching a silhouette come towards him. Out of the many trying to kill each other, this gaunt figure comes for him. He dashes out of the fog, taking Lisa with him.
Soon the pair make it out of the fog, but not the hell. The streets have erupted into vicious and blood-filled

brawls. A dome-like fire incases them in the city. The madness like the virus has spread. It's not just opposing ideals clashing. It's everyday citizens, now tearing through their streets. People with nothing rampage through luxurious homes, taking everything; some are forcefully dragged out of their homes, executed feet away from their door. Fire consumes a church, making it crumble brick by brick. Statues of saints with their hands in prayer have rope lassoed around them then toppled down, shattering on the pavement.

Someone dawning all-black plunges a knife through the throat of an officer. A Javier supporter nearly beats a person draped in black to death. Random people, not belonging to any side, begin pepper-spraying each other and throwing rotten food. Jack turns around; the striking figure is right on their tail. He grabs Lisa and runs through the melting streets.

More cars are set on fire, even more explode. The front of a building gives out, collapsing. People near the building have debris split onto them, trapping them underneath. Jack and Lisa move out of the way as the building comes down. An older man dressed in a black shirt reading: *Justice for Debora* quickly latches onto Lisa. He tightly grips her shoulders, screaming in her face, with his crazed bug-eyes. She tries to squirm from his grasp.

"OPPRESSOR! OPPRESSOR!" the crazed man shouts in Lisa's face. She continues to squirm, but his grip is too firm. She swings her leg, hitting the man between the legs. In pain, he finally let go, holding his bruised crotch.

Jack swings a mean right hook into the crazed man's

128

skull knocking him down. The man stays on the pavement, weak. Jack begins to beat him, launching his knuckles into the side of the man's head. Lisa turns her head; the imposing figure is nearly reaching them. Lisa pulls Jack away.

Jack and Lisa continue to sprint. They duck as a man with a flamethrower shoots out fire from the top of a car. Bullets zip through his head, sending him down. His brains fly over Jack and Lisa, yet they keep moving. A police officer is having his skull caved in by the foot soldiers of a lost idea. The pair keep going. An elderly lady is quickly surrounded by an angry mob dressed in black. Soon they beat her to death. The two continue to run. Neighbor's turn on one another, screaming, cursing, brutally fighting each other. Still, the couple keeps running. The pair try to run through the destruction, the madness, and the savagery—the couple run with no point. There is no escaping a falling society. There is no out without a shred of decency. There is no more hiding, no more running. It's caught up with everyone, and everybody pays the price. Everyone has encased themselves in impervious bubbles, driving them to the highest levels of insanity. Some embrace the chaos, celebrating the collapse of their city.

Amid the mayhem, Lisa spots a dimly lit alley; she swiftly grips Jack's hand, pulling him towards it. The couple making their way across the street are nearly hit by a runaway car. The wild car speeds swerving into a crowd of people, killing them. The two continue to take shelter in the pale lit alley. Inside, the graffiti decorates the close walls. A single light shines above Jack and Lisa, both glad they are out of the chaos. The pair covered in blood stains and ash. Tired, they sit on the filthy ground.

129

"What do we do? It's like we're trapped," asks Lisa, panicked.

"I don't know. Everyone's lost their goddamn mind." Jack pauses, "Maybe we should wait here until morning. Things will probably cool down by then."

"You really think we have until morning? Look at what's going on; I think we should keep moving."

"Where?"

"I don't know. I do know; we'll be in a lot more danger if we're just sitting ducks!"

"Goddamnit! Those damn fools…"

"Hey, look, we just need to focus on surviving the night. Okay?"

Lisa gently places her soft hand on Jack's cheek. He turns to look at her. He's lost in those emerald eyes. Looking deep into them gives him everything he needs.

"Yeah. You're right. I'm sorry, we just need to keep moving. Let's rest up for a few more minutes; then we'll move. Hopefully, we can make it to a hospital. It'll probably be safe there."

"I'll be with you, every step of the way.", Lisa says, holding Jack's hand.

"I won't let go," replies Jack, kissing the back of her hand.

The pair sit alone in the alley. Until a faint sound in the distance catches their attention, they both rise to their feet. Jack slides Lisa behind him, shielding her with his body. The striking figure has caught up with them. Jack's eyes narrow on the figure walking into the light. Lisa tries to peek behind Jack.

"What do you want!" Jack yells in frustration.

The figure does not answer; he steps forward. A scrawny tall young man dressed in black comes into the light. His shirt reads: *ACAB*; below it is a picture of a sickle and hammer crossing. Jack is astonished by the young man's age. He can't be more than twenty-one years old. The kid's eyes nearly pop out of his head, making Jack all the more nervous.

"What do you want?" asks Jack.

The kid doesn't answer. Annoyed, Jack walks towards him, about to knock him down. Suddenly, the kid pulls out a snub nose from his jacket pocket. With a tweaking hand, he points it at Jack. Slowly Jack raises his hands. Lisa lets out a little scream in fear.

"It's okay, just stay behind me.", says Jack calmly to Lisa.

Lisa captures the attention of the kid; he points the gun at her.

"Hey, keep it on me! You want me, right? Keep it on Me!"
"Jack, no, don't!"
"It's okay; we're all cool. Just let her go, take me."

Jack keeps a cool head while tears stream down Lisa's soft cheeks. The gun is staring down at Jack again. His eyes glance at the kid's trigger finger; it's shaky. His

131

entire hand is trembling. He hasn't pulled back the hammer yet.

"Let her go. You want me; I'm yours. Just let her go.!"

The kid's eyes glance back and forth between Jack's stern look and Lisa's sobbing face. Jack can feel the kid growing more nervous, feeling his uncertainty.

"Goddamnit, take me!"
"Gavin Bishop sends his regards."

Quickly closing his eyes, his hand still wobbly, the kid pulls the trigger. BANG! Petrified, Jack had closed his eyes before his coming death. Opening them, he realizes he's still standing. In shock, Lisa looks down at her torso; blood smears through her shirt. She collapses. Jack catches her before she hits the ground.

"NO!"

Jack looks up towards the young man. The kid's eyes widened. With the snub nose still in his hands, he quickly points it back at Jack, pulling the trigger. It jams—wrathful Jack right hooks the kid in the corner of his jaw, the snub nose falls to the ground. Jack pins the kid against the wall, violently slamming him against it.

"YOU COWARDASS BASTARD!" screams Jack in the kid's face.

Jack's head swells like a balloon, filled with rage.

Fear pumps through the kid as Jack glares at him with seething eyes. The kid feels the hard brick hitting his skull as Jack continues to throw him against the wall. Vexed, Jack throws the kid on the ground, pinning him down. The kid tries to squirm. Jack aggressively punches the kid in the face. The kid's nose breaks. Some of his teeth crack. His mouth bleeds. Jack's knuckles now painted with the kid's blood. The snub nose is only inches away from the kid's reach. He tries to grab it, but Jack is too strong. Grabbing the snub nose, he presses it against the kid's forehead. Jack wraps his finger around the trigger, pulling it. The gun jams gun. Infuriated, Jack starts beating the kid's head with the handle of the gun. Rapidly Jack whips the pistol against the kid's head. Just as he is about to hit the kid again, he stops. Brain hangs from the grip; the kid's skull is caved-in.

Disgusted, Jack throws the gun to the side. He hears a slight whimpering from Lisa. He rushes to her, holding her in his arms. Her eyes stare mindlessly up at Jack. Her hand slowly moves up his arm, trying to make it to his face. Jack grips her cold hand, pressing it against his cheek. His eyes puff up, tears run down his face.

"Stay with me! Please don't go!"

Lisa tries to make out words, but she's slipping away. Jack watches her eyes roll back, and lids close. He continues to hold her hand, suddenly feeling it go still; Jack trembles in anguish. He scrambles, sliding his hand behind Lisa's head.

"Hey! No! No! Stay with me!"

She doesn't respond. Having little options, Jack turns to face out the alley, the chaos still brewing. Carrying Lisa in his arms, he rises before rushing back into the streets. Jack running through the smoke-filled madness surrounding him, buildings collapse, eaten by the fire. With the police vanquished, the people freely slaughter each other, some pillaging homes and stores leaving no survivors. Blood trickles through the streets. Above, the night sky is clouded in thick grey smoke.

Continuing to run, Jack glances down at Lisa's motionless face. Scrunching his face, he pushes himself to run faster. Passing through the different kinds of smoke, Jack coughs. Soon he feels his thighs burn. His legs start to buckle. His arms are growing restless. His heart is jumping; it's nearly popping out of his chest. His breath can't keep up. In the distance, he can see the tip of the hospital tower. Its bright neon sign shines through the thick smoke. Jack isn't far; he decides to push himself. On the verge of collapse, Jack is only a couple of blocks away. After an hour and a half, perhaps Lisa could still be saved. Jack rounds a corner, abruptly, he stops running. His eyes widen, tears fall from the corner of his eyes before dropping to his knees. The fire rises in his reflection. The first floor of the hospital has collapsed. Flames burn the second floor, slowly making their way up; some run inside, taking supplies, avoiding those crawling out. The doctors, nurses try to help the patients out of the building but are swarmed by the uncontrollable mobs.

Jack sobs holding Lisa tight in his arms. With tears in his eyes, he looks at her. Gently he brushes the loose hairs out of her face. He can feel her warm blood soak through his clothes, drying on his flesh. He pulls her in

134

close, staring at her closed eyes, hoping they'd spring back open. Tears continue to stream down his face as he holds her snugly in his arms. Moments of rage and hate flow through him, but sorrow hangs over him. Jack sits still, in total defeat. The hoards of people around him run with madness guiding them. The structures around all of them crumble. They all have fallen.

24

Morning. Faint clouds of smoke float towards a gloomy sky; the sun barely shines. Ash lightly falls onto the ground. Buildings once towered over the streets left in ruin. Buried underneath the collapsed structure lay crisp corpses. There's nothing but rubble left. Cars parked along the roads are charred shells. Homeless camps burned into nothing. A young woman with bright neon green hair is draped in dry blood and ash. A metal rod pierces through her thigh, forcing her to sit on a pile of corpses. She cries out in tears with only the dead to keep her company. The few medic's, police, and firefighters, who haven't been killed or quit, walk through the ruined streets searching for survivors. People, who survived the night huddle together, glad the nightmare is over. Religious leaders hum prayers as they pass through the streets, feeling the blood and broken glass behind them.

Javier, accompanied by his wife, daughters, and private security, searches through the ruined streets. Frantically they look for Lisa. Javier doesn't know where to start; everything is left in shambles. Suddenly, he sees a figure in the distance. He gets a better view as the person walks closer. His eyes widen, and his jaw drops.

His wife gasps, putting her hand to her mouth. Their daughters watch in panic. Jack walks alone in the street, still holding Lisa in his arms. Stained with blood and covered with ash, Jack remains stoic. He has nothing in him anymore. Lisa's sister's bursts into tears, their mother wraps them in her arms. She tries to put on a brave face, but she breaks down with them. Jack stands in front of Javier, who is speechless. He makes little noise, though streams come down from the corner of his eyes. Javier hesitates to walk towards Jack. His hands tremble as he reaches for his daughter. Javier carefully takes Lisa's cold body into his arms. Within seconds he falls to his knees, quietly weeping. His family gathers behind him, surrounding him. Though their blood was not the same, the stinging pain ripped through them. They mourned together. Jack just watched them suffer with a blank expression on his face. He had seen a family once stand on the shoulders of angels, now plummet into the dark. Looking at their faces, Jack could feel the anguish they felt. He could feel the pain run through Javier as he held his daughter for the last time. The same feeling of sorrow that overcame him the night before amplified watching the family suffer. He lowered his head, feeling a sense of guilt for their pain.

A small crowd of journalists, who were brave enough to come down from their towers, walked towards Javier. They said nothing as they surrounded the Valénica family, filming their pain for millions to view. Javier, a man who showed the people his charming smile and assertive demeanor, was now broken. He was at his weakest, which was profitable. Their camera couldn't capture the love they shared for Lisa; their audiences wouldn't have believed it. Jack knew they would probably spin the story against him, and their audience would believe it; it was their depraved nature. More people started surrounding them; Javier's security moved in closer, keeping a close watch.

Through lies and stoking the flames, people got what they wanted. They just didn't expect it to hit them so hard when everything came to blow. The people's crusades in the name of peace and tranquility had ended in death and destruction. It's how they always end. People are just too naive to think otherwise. Their good intentions did nothing but pave a path to hell. They all paid the price.

As the camera's and phones kept filming, rage replaced the sorrow that was going through Jack. He could feel the lenses stare at him, recording his every expression. He didn't know who he was angriest with, them or himself. He looked down at Lisa, her skin pale, body cold, and lifeless. She made him realize there were things beyond politics; there was life to be lived, avoiding the consumption of trivial matters. Adopting politics as theology in search of meaning was fruitless, leaving pain and emptiness. She recognized this long before he had, but it was too late for him by that time. Through the time they spent together, she saw him for who he was and loved him, a quality that was lost by the journalist recording him. They had strived against the truth. Looking at the journalist, then back at the Valénica family, he could no longer hold in his anger.

"YOU DID THIS!" Jack snapped at the cameras, "We all did this...for what, utopia? Look around. Does this look like utopia? We all lost."

Jack knelt in front of the Valénica family, mourning with them, sharing in their pain. He closed his eyes for a moment. His vivid memories of people slaughtering each other remained with him. The gunshot that took his love would haunt him forever. He had survived the night, realizing people were not good. People trapped themselves in fear, confining themselves in dark paranoia. Anyone who offered them a glimpse into the light, they hated and censored, refusing to come out from the shadows.

EPILOGUE

Some months had passed since the horrific night of chaos. Despite the destruction, people still believed to inflict pain was necessary to be understood. Anybody who challenged the idea was exiled. Change was coming; people demanded peace with a heavy hand. Though it led to more poverty, fear, rage, and destroyed cities, it was essential to the road of tranquility.

Gavin was charged and investigated for his crimes. However, because of his friends, he was stripped of the title: politician; forced to live as a nameless wealthy man. Javier had won the election. He only stayed in office for a short time before leaving. The memory of lowering his daughter's coffin into a grave was too fresh in his mind. Javier, along with his family, abandoned the ranch. Dan Donahue turned broke; without Javier, SNN was nothing. Javier and Jack never reach out to each other after the funeral. They had shared enough pain for one lifetime. They faded from each other's existence.

Another established politician, who was power hungry and concerned with his own pockets, voiced his support for the people. Behind the veil, he was an old crook with dementia. The people believing him to be their savior voted him in office. He repaid them with nothing, except a prolonged shut down of the state blaming the virus. Nothing changed. He made sure to protect corporations, powerful tech companies and let the people starve. The government, even the police, abandoned the people. They did not understand why they suffered; they had made the right choice. So, they rioted and tore down everything stable because they wanted to see a reflection of their insanity. Reality was no match for their metallic bubbles.

Jack stayed away from the cities, where society had been collapsing. He confined himself to his cottage surrounded by nature, isolated from the public. Left alone, he thought he would be pleased. The loss of Lisa still tormented him. He looked for a cure to his ailment in bottles, both day and night. Sometimes he hoped to drink himself to death. Occasionally he covered news pieces, but it all disgusted him. Jack learned to live off the land, keeping to himself. He grew a distrust for people. Having seen their nature and abilities, he wanted nothing from them.

One would think a sense of decency would have prevailed through tragedy. Instead, everybody looked at each other as judges of morality, too advanced to be bothered with modesty. In this age, there was no humanity; people traded passions of life for politics. Trivial matters came before art, love, and lovemaking. People foolishly worshiped shallow status'. No one cared for real good, only presentation at its highest quality, resulting in a warped and perverted morality. Everyone had to be reminded the world was ending and they were to blame. To live in peace was profane. With vast information and refusing to speak with others, people lived in darkness.

The truth is dead, and we killed it.

Micheal Romo is a Southern California native born to write and has been since a young age. He self-published his first novella, Whistleblower, at the age of 21.

To keep up with his latest projects, follow him on,

Instagram: @micheal_romco
Twitter: @MichealRomCo

www.ingramcontent.com/pod-product-compliance
Lightning Source LLC
Chambersburg PA
CBHW070335130626
46556CB00007B/2865